I0627866

Scout

Killers Inc #5

Charity Parkerson

Punk & Sissy Publications

Copyright

—Warning: This book is intended for readers over the age of 18. Some of my books contain allusions to past abuse and trauma.

Contents

About the Author

Introduction

THE MOMENT CLAY WAS old enough to help guard the Bosi home, he was trained as a soldier. He's seen criminals come and go. He's never met anyone like Scout.

As Killers Inc.'s scout, Scout has two areas of expertise. He's the eagle eyes of the group, and he can shoot faster and more accurately than more than ninety-five percent of the population. That's it. That's all Scout has. Since meeting Clay, he's smiled even more than usual. The best part is the happiness isn't faked. Scout didn't notice what was happening to him until he saw Clay stare at someone else with lust in his eyes. Those longing looks were supposed to be his. He's never felt further out of his comfort zone.

For nearly his entire life, Clay has been surrounded by crime. He doesn't care what anyone does. All Clay knows is he wants to be with someone sane and kind. Unfortunately, his position with the Bosi family has made it hard to meet anyone nice. Since the Killers Inc. group joined the compound, teasing him with a life he never thought he would have, Clay isn't sure what he's looking for any longer. But he's positive something is happening to him, and he has never been more confused.

Scout is the fifth book in Charity Parkerson's Killers Inc. series, where hired assassins and their ilk find the love that finally saves them. These are best enjoyed when read in order.

Chapter One

THE ACRES OF WOODED land where the Bosi property was located sometimes felt secluded as hell. For years, Clay had trailed through every inch, checking for security breaches. Those strolls had always been one of his favorite assignments in the day. Since the Agafonov family combined their lives with the Bosi family, his walks had been shortened, if he got to go at all. One Agafonov brother, Tracker, was a god of technology. He had installed the most badass of high-tech security equipment that money could buy and ran it all with ease. Truthfully, he had rendered most of Beau's live-in staff useless. Now they simply served as an army slash personal bodyguards. While his job still wasn't a bad one, he missed the solitude and peace of zigzagging through nature half of the day. Now Clay felt like he had to look busy most of the day. It was kind of stressful.

As part of his new daily routine, Clay cut through the back hallways of the main house. He did what he always did—he prayed for a few hours of no one else bursting into the kitchen. Chef Fabrice was the master of his domain. He wouldn't let just anyone sit with him while he worked. While there was a kitchen table for people to sit, Fabrice quickly shuffled most people toward the formal dining room. He didn't like people in his space. Clay and barely a handful of others were the only exceptions.

Since Fabrice and Clay had grown up together inside the Bosi home, and they were the same age, they had naturally been glued at the hip since day one. Clay enjoyed spending his shift in Fabrice's bubble. Maybe he was just lazy, but his job was kind of boring.

Clay peeked inside the kitchen, ensuring it was empty, before slipping inside. There were other kitchen staff members always bouncing around, working on baked goods and whatnot. They paid no mind to Clay. Fabrice was their boss. If he said Clay could come in and do whatever he wanted, then that was what happened.

The opulent kitchen had every toy a true chef would kill to have. Black stainless steel appliances littered every space. A huge flow of gorgeously patterned backsplash made the entire place easier for the cleaning staff to keep sparkling. Delicious smells wafted all around him. Fresh bread and apple pie smelled like coming home. The luminous smile that greeted him warmed the air. Fabrice's jet-black hair and light-blue eyes were as familiar to Clay as his own reflection.

"At last. I saved you pie."

"Hey." Clay raced Fabrice's way and lifted him off his feet. "It's my friend." He loudly kissed Fabrice's cheek while Fabrice fought to get away and wipe his cheek.

"Brute."

Clay's face hurt from how big he smiled as he set Fabrice aside. "You love me. Where's the pie?" He rubbed his hands together. Clay really wasn't hungry. One of these days, he would be as big as a house with the way Fabrice spoiled him, especially now that they had shortened his daily walks.

The way Fabrice glowed with happiness proved how fake his struggles had been as he brought a small plate and fork to the table. "Limoncello?"

Clay clutched his chest dramatically. "It's like you don't even know me." He dropped his hands. "That stuff tastes like floor cleaner. I'll grab some tea."

A snort burst from Fabrice as he moved to make the tea. "Drunk a lot of floor cleaner in your life, have you?"

Clay really would have made his own tea, but it was Fabrice's kitchen. He didn't like his things being touched.

"Probably. You were there. I was a terror."

"Were?" Fabrice looked his way with raised eyebrows and shock sketching his features. "You're a menace now."

Clay chuckled as he shoved a bite of apple pie in his mouth.

Fabrice set the glass of tea next to Clay's plate on the counter. "You—"

Henry strolled into the kitchen, cutting off Fabrice and catching Clay mid-bite. "Why am I not surprised to find you here?"

Damn. Henry was Beau Bosi's partner and Clay's boss. A groan rang through Clay's head. The guy had an uncanny ability to always bust Clay every time he went to visit Fabrice. "I'm on—"

Henry swiped a hand through the air. His brown eyes practically glowed with impatience. "Yeah. I don't care. Go pack a bag. You're heading to Hawaii ahead of the family. I need you to sweep the property before the rest of us join you next week. You know what to look for. It's your responsibility to make sure the place is one hundred percent secure before Beau and Kylo get there. Understood?"

Clay gave him a sharp nod. "On it." Like he would complain about a week longer at the compound in Hawaii. He had never been sent to handle security ahead of time.

Henry's gaze swept Fabrice's way. "You're still needed here. You'll leave with the family next week."

"Oui, Monsieur."

Henry focused on Clay again. "The plane will be ready in an hour."

Damn. That gave him barely any time to pack. Thankfully, he had already started since he had to be prepared for six weeks in the tropics. Seven now. "I'll be there."

Henry smiled. If Clay wasn't mistaken, the gesture had a devilish edge. "Have fun."

Clay didn't know how to respond. While he planned to make some time for fun, he didn't think he should admit that to his boss. He ended up just nodding and hoping that was enough.

Henry strolled out without another word.

Clay and Fabrice exchanged a glance.

Fabrice broke first. "You should hurry. It's at least half an hour to get to the airstrip."

A smile exploded across Clay's face. He couldn't help it. Clay was going to Hawaii for a whole week alone. He hadn't truly had a vacation in years. "I'm gone." He shoveled the last of the pie into his mouth and chugged the tea. Clay gave Fabrice another messy kiss on his cheek.

Fabrice shoved at his chest. "Oui. I love you too. Get lost."

With a loud laugh, Clay skipped from the kitchen like a kid and headed through the back halls to his bedroom. He would be on the beach by the end of the day. Clay couldn't fucking wait.

There were no good radio stations in this area. Scout hadn't wanted to pair his phone with a car that didn't belong to him. There was no fucking way he would make the thirty-minute drive without tunes. He tapped the screen on the dash to get started. Clay came through the door into the garage, fighting with two suitcases.

Scout honked.

Clay jumped as if a dog bit his ass.

Scout couldn't fight his smile as Clay's glare swung his way.

Scout chuckled as he waved for Clay to join him. When Clay took a step in his direction without his luggage, Scout rolled down the window. "I'm your chariot."

As Clay lugged his bags to the car, he looked torn between confused and nervous. They made half a second's worth of eye contact before Clay skittered past to get away. This time, when Scout chuckled, the laugh sounded as dangerous as he was. Just three nights prior, they had kissed. Scout was pretty certain he had made his intentions known. But the way Clay had kissed him—like one good fuck from him would ruin Scout for everyone—did not match the bending-over-backwards-to-avoid-him Clay had done since. Scout was about to ruin all that for Clay. There was no escaping him now.

Clay slipped into the passenger seat. A loud metal song Scout loved blared through the radio before Clay closed the door.

Scout's gaze shot toward the dash. Clay's phone had connected automatically. It seemed they had the same taste in music. That was good. Now Scout knew exactly which playlist he would use when he let Clay bend him over the first solid piece of furniture they found.

"Sorry about that." Clay turned the radio down. He met Scout's stare. His eyes slid away, as if he couldn't look at Scout directly. Scout knew what he saw. All the hunger he felt when he was with Clay had to show on his face. "I forgot what I'd been listening to when I got home yesterday."

If Clay wanted to talk about mundane things, they would. "It's cool. I couldn't find a good station."

Clay nodded. "You won't out here. We're kind of in a dead area."

Scout tapped his fingers on the steering wheel as he waited for Clay to put on his seatbelt. "So, is this the car you drive when you go out?"

Clay laughed. "Yeah, dude. It's my car."

The realization embarrassed him a little, and Scout wasn't one to feel flustered. He brazened it out. "Oops. Henry threw me the keys." Scout tapped his fingers again, hoping Clay took the hint.

Clay still made no move to buckle up.

He couldn't take it. "Seatbelt."

"I don't wear seatbelts."

Scout's eyebrows rose. "You do when I drive."

They held each other's stare, trying to wait each other out.

Scout tapped his fingers again.

Clay sighed heavily, but he buckled his seatbelt.

"Good boy." Scout put the car in reverse. His attention moved to driving while he looked for any reason to talk to Clay. "Why don't you like seatbelts? In this day and age, with all the knowledge we have, it's kind of a dumbass move. Not that I'm calling you dumb. We both know you're not, so why make that choice?"

"I'm not trying to be bullheaded. When I drive, I wear it." Heavy laughter laced Clay's words. "I was in a bad car accident two years ago. Another guard and I were on an errand. A huge truck steered into our lane and hit us head-on. He was driving and uninjured. The seatbelt broke my collarbone. Now, when I wear one, it puts too much pressure on a spot that already hurts ninety percent of the time."

"Is the seatbelt hurting right now?" Scout automatically glanced Clay's way to check if he told the truth.

A small smile touched Clay's lips. "Always."

Scout pulled to the shoulder of the road and put the car in park. He didn't hang around for any questions. Scout removed his shirt as he circled the car. The moment he opened Clay's door, he expected to get the third degree. Instead,

Clay sat quietly, looking like he trusted Scout completely.

Scout wrapped his shirt around the seatbelt, padding it right where it fell across Clay's collarbone. "I'll get it back from you when we get to the airstrip." He purposely avoided Clay's gaze, but he felt the man's gorgeous hazel eyes eating him alive. The moment Scout focused on Clay, the air froze in his lungs.

Clay's gaze moved over Scout's chest. His expression screamed he would do bad things to Scout and do them very well. When he met Scout's stare, he didn't look embarrassed to get caught ogling him. "Love the ink."

"Thanks." Scout straightened and closed the door. Confusion ruled him. He was flustered. Scout never got bashful in any way. Something about the way Clay looked at him was different. He hadn't learned how to deal with normal situations like this one. Lust, he got. Even unrequited desire was in his wheelhouse, but there was something new when he was with Clay. He didn't know how to handle this. He climbed back behind the wheel.

"Thank you for this. It helps."

The pressure in Scout's chest eased. He was being ridiculous. When he looked Clay's way, he was back to being bewildered. Clay was a sexy guy with his blond hair and full lips. He had one dimple when he smiled, for fuck's sake. The man was irresistible. There was no reason Scout couldn't manage him.

"I'll buy you one of those seatbelt cushion things."

Clay's mouth lifted in one corner. That was it. Scout was hard as stone. He had to get back to driving before he accidentally sprang. Scout was named Scout for a reason. He had an eagle eye for details and nuances. Clay was more complicated than most. Sometimes he seemed shy, and at other times, he looked like a man with a plan. Like with the tattoo thing, Scout had no clue if Clay had been legit checking out his ink or if he had truly seen lust. Maybe he was seeing what he wanted.

Scout mused about it for the rest of the drive. At the privately run airport for personal jets, Scout parked inside the hangar where the guards indicated.

When he opened his door, Clay stopped him and handed him back his shirt. "Thanks for the ride."

It hit Scout. Clay thought this was just Scout doing him a favor. "You know I'm coming with you, right? I'm the best at what I do. Beau asked me to go with you and make sure everything was totally secure."

Clay's closed expression gave nothing away. "Oh." He climbed from the car.

Scout chuckled as he did the same. Maybe Clay confused him, but he heard the tone of that "oh." Clay knew he was in danger, and he was right.

Chapter Two

WHOA, BOY. CLAY WAS in trouble. Until three nights ago, Clay hadn't thought there would ever be anything between Scout and him beyond the amazing friendship they had built. Scout had been teaching Clay how to shoot the way he had learned in the spy program: fast and accurate. It was a lot of fun. They had done a ton of laughing together. But Scout hadn't seemed to look at Clay in any sort of romantic light, as far as Clay could tell... and then Scout had kissed him. Scout had been born into a Russian program that trained spies to be the perfect robots. They had a special skill honed to flawless while also being taught how to fit in with any situation. Scout didn't talk about those days. Clay didn't ask. They simply enjoyed each other's company. Then Zeus kissed Clay first, bringing out all sorts of feelings, and Clay had gotten a little obsessed with the guy who was absolutely God's favorite. Zeus was sexy in every fucking way imaginable. As hard as he tried not to, because there was no future there, Clay always found himself watching Zeus, hoping for something, anything to happen. Scout busted him studying Zeus. That became the first and only time Clay heard Scout speak about the place they had been raised. Not about his time in that hell, but Zeus'. His words taught Clay a lesson more thoroughly than any rejection ever would. Zeus hadn't kissed him for any reason beyond that was just who he was. If Clay fed the beast the program created, Zeus would bite, and Clay would get hurt. Clay couldn't say if the speech had actually deterred him in any way, but he knew now he had no real shot. Except then Scout kissed him, and that move turned him on his head. The last three nights, he hadn't done much beyond thinking about the last few months they had spent together.

Now, Clay couldn't stop picturing Scout walking toward their waiting plane. His hips moved like a man's who knew his worth. They swayed with a swagger of confidence. The muscles in Scout's back—and there were a lot of them—had flexed as he put his shirt back on. Clay still wanted to whimper at the loss of that sight. He knew now exactly how Scout would look walking away from his bed. *That* was what getting hurt would truly look like. Clay understood the truth now. None of these men would ever be his.

Clay carefully scanned each room of Beau's vacation home. He was determined not to miss a single inch. Clay wouldn't have people getting hurt. This home was a lot more welcoming than the compound where they lived. It was still massive, though. The place had been built especially for Beau's husband, Kylo. Kylo was sweet, wild, and everything Beau wasn't. Thankfully, Beau knew it and did everything he could to protect the amazing miracle he had been granted. Kylo turned the hardened criminal's life around. He looked at Beau and saw a person no one else did. It was kind of beautiful. Clay wouldn't let any harm come to Kylo. He was a huge blessing to their house. This property being for Kylo made it kind of fun to search. The place had a kid's playroom. Kylo was a Little, which was a lifestyle Clay didn't understand, but he didn't judge. There was a dance studio. Kylo was a former ballet dancer. Apparently, he had once been a professional, dancing in several huge productions, including a run on Broadway. Kylo still loved to dance, and Beau encouraged him. This entire house was a monument or some sort of playground just for Kylo. Still, there had to be dozens of rooms to accommodate Beau's army. Safety came first, and Beau had trusted Clay to do this sweep. That was a hell of an ego boost. While everyone always said Beau thought highly of him, Clay never put too much stock into it. Beau could turn cold in a way Clay had never seen elsewhere. It was best just to stay in his lane.

Seven weeks in the tropics. He rubbed his hands together in his mind. An entire team would be here. Clay would get plenty of time off to get into trouble. Fabrice would be here too. They always found something fun to do.

"All the cameras are working fine."

Clay nearly jumped out of his skin at Scout's silent appearance. He spun.

Scout looked amused by his reaction.

Clay narrowed his eyes. When he thought of something to say, he would really tear into Scout for always startling him.

"Okay. Real talk." Scout didn't look the least bit contrite. "Why are you so jumpy around me all the sudden? You've also been avoiding me since that kiss. We're supposed to be friends. I thought you understood I was only making a point."

"Okay." Clay's response came out sounding as insulted as he was. That had been a real asshole thing to say.

Scout smiled. "For about the first ten seconds I'd been making a point. After that, it was because you're sexy and I wanted to kiss you."

Clay didn't know if he was appeased or not. "Okay."

Scout sighed like he couldn't be more tired of anyone. "There's really no winning with you. You kissed me back—like this attraction goes both ways." He motioned between them. "Then you ran for your life and didn't talk to me again until you had no choice. Now your expression screams I've insulted you. Fuck, dude. This is about to be a really uncomfortable week of working together if you don't learn how to communicate."

A smile exploded across Clay's face. "To be fair, Fabrice and I raised each other, so I really didn't have anyone to teach me how to talk things out."

Scout cocked his head. "Hmm." He sounded stumped as he studied Clay. "I'll keep that in mind. I'll double-check the security system." Scout walked away, leaving Clay even more perplexed. Scout being willing to communicate was super-hot. Maybe he was even more interested than he realized.

The news that Fabrice and Clay raised each other was a bit of a surprise. He hadn't thought to ask about Clay's past. All those nights of shooting lessons had been more playful than anything. Scout never pried because he didn't want anyone poking into his past life. He had another option.

Scout shut himself in the security room and risked looking crazy by calling Tracker.

Tracker answered on the first ring, like he was scared something had happened. "Are you okay?"

Scout supposed he kind of deserved that. He only called Tracker when there was a problem on the job. Otherwise, the guy was right down the hall. He could walk to talk to him quicker than Scout could find his contact info in his phone.

"Yeah. I'm good. Sorry to scare you."

"No, it's good. I guess I'm feeling out of sorts with you being so far away. You know me. If it isn't stressing me out, then I'm not controlling the situation."

Scout chuckled. "At least you're self-aware. I need a favor."

Tracker didn't let him down. "Shoot. I'm free and bored."

Scout shook his head. Tracker wasn't the best at doing nothing. The techie of their group had a big brain that needed stimulation. "Can you send a dossier on Clay? He said something today about his past that's got me curious. You know me; I'm nosy."

Tracker laughed. "Yeah. Me too. It just so happens I created a file for everyone living with Beau when we first arrived. I won't take any chances with our family."

"I figured you had things under control. You always do. You're the real protector of our group."

He heard Tracker clicking away on his computer. "That's high praise coming from you."

Scout got it. He was the eyes. The first line of defense and the last resort. It was Scout's job to ensure they never walked into a trap. He was also the one who neutralized the problem if anyone slipped past all their defenses.

"Dossier sent."

"Thanks, man. I'll repay the favor any-time you like."

Tracker snorted, and the call discon-nected.

Scout chuckled as he moved to sit at the desk. Scout turned his back to the room, facing the huge monitor with all the camera views. If Clay checked, it would look like he still worked on the camera system. He got comfortable and opened the file. The beginning was pretty stan-dard stuff; still, Scout laughed when he saw Tracker had even included Clay's height. Tracker was definitely on top of everything.

Clay Bernardi.

That was very Italian and heightened Scout's curiosity. *Twenty-five.*

"Damn." His curse sounded shocked even to Scout's ears. He had known Clay looked young, but that was still seven years younger than Scout.

Five-foot-eleven.

Scout nodded. He had figured as much. Clay was only slightly shorter than Scout's six-one.

Born in Italy. Unknown parentage.

Whoa. Scout couldn't believe even Tracker didn't know Clay's parents.

Brought to the U.S. at four years old by a sex-trafficking ring. Rescued by the Russian mob boss, Zander Kapra. His organization, The Kapra Foundation, named and re-homed Clay with Beau and Tabitha Bosi. Where he has lived since.

That explained the missing details. As good as Tracker was, Zander Kapra was not one to toy with. He likely had bots in place that triggered if anyone searched for details on anyone in his sphere.

"You know. Anything you wanted to know about me; you could've just asked. I thought you preferred communication."

Scout startled so hard, he had to catch himself before he toppled from the chair. "Fuck!" He called himself under control. "I didn't hear you come in."

A small, humor-filled smile hovered on Clay's lips. "I'll bet." He grabbed a nearby rolling chair. After pulling it to Scout's side, he sat. His hazel eyes held no animosity. All Scout saw was kindness. "It's not like I have some secret, shameful roots. I'm also nowhere near the only rescue living at Beau's. Zander and he have a gentleman's contract of sorts. They work together, using their powerful positions to deter unwanted illegal activities."

Scout was all the way fascinated. "You said Fabrice and you raised each other. Is he a rescue as well?"

A sexy chuckle fell from Clay's perfect lips, and goosebumps skittered across Scout's skin. He was adorable. "No. He's Pierre's grandson."

"The retired chef?"

Clay nodded. "It would probably take you weeks to find out where everyone is from and how they got there. I'm one of the lucky ones. I can't remember anything about my life before Beau."

Scout leaned closer. He realized something. Scout could talk to Clay all night. He kind of wanted to do that. "What was it like growing up in that home as a child who wasn't his?"

Clay shrugged. "Not that I have anything to compare it to, but normal, I guess. Fabrice and I aren't that much younger than Beau's kids. We had the same private tutor. The same nanny. We played at Tabitha's feet. Anytime she took Boone and Banks on vacation, she took us too. She was an absolute treasure before the drugs and alcohol turned her into a stranger. I watched the whole family mourn her while she was still alive. There were several years when that house turned into a battlefield. Then she passed, and things got even darker until Kylo."

Scout chuckled. "I'm sure that was a breath of fresh air."

"It really was. Beau was never like a father figure or anything like that. Fabrice and I were kept completely away from the inner workings of the Bosi family until I started training for my current position. Not to say we were treated as outsiders or anything. Pierre is the one who's always acted like my dad."

"So Fabrice is like a brother to you?"

"Exactly!"

Thank God. Scout had worried about that one.

Clay kept talking, unknowingly easing Scout's fears of competing with someone who had been in Clay's life for years. "We used to fight like siblings, and I got punished the same as he did. In fact, Pierre used to ground us, but we were each other's best friends, and we lived under the same roof. What was he actually grounding us from?" Clay laughed as he spoke, and Scout couldn't look away.

"I like you."

They fell silent and held each other's stare at Scout's sudden admission.

He didn't take it back. "Giving you those lessons has been one of my best decisions." Scout purposely didn't say if he meant as a friend or more. If all Clay wanted was friendship, Scout would take it.

Clay's eyes always fascinated Scout. It was like his whole soul shone through them, and it was beautiful. "I like you too." Clay slapped his knees and stood.

"Well, I guess I need to get back to it. I don't know about you, but I really don't want to sleep in a house that hasn't been thoroughly secured."

"Agreed." Scout stood too. He wouldn't call Clay out for running again. Scout saw him now. Clay hadn't been mistreated. In fact, he had been given a hell of a great life compared to where he would've ended up if Beau hadn't taken him in. But Clay hadn't walked away with no issues. It was in Scout's DNA to read people. Clay feared the fuck out of rejection. Despite his understanding that he was a rescue, and not a child of Beau's, he still felt unworthy of love. Scout totally got it. They were the same. Scout doubted anyone could ever love someone like him.

Chapter Three

TWO DAYS IN HAWAII felt like a lifetime. Clay still had almost the full seven weeks to go. Working next to Scout every day, talking and laughing, was absolute hell. Clay noticed everything about him, from his smell to how sexy his smile looked when his eyes swam with genuine happiness. Clay wanted more every day. There was only one way to survive. He had to get out and find something else to do with his time. As shitty as it seemed, Clay waited until Scout was busy to grab one of Beau's cars from the massive garage and head out. Even though he always wore his seatbelt when he drove, Clay still smiled as he strapped in, thinking about Scout's outrage over him not wearing one. The farther he got from the estate, the more his chest hurt. Feeling any sort of way was ridiculous. He also really hated going out alone. Once upon a time, he had dragged poor Shadow out to the club after he had gotten shot. That was how much he hated doing things alone. Of course, the Shadow thing was a bit of a different story. Under any other circumstances, he would have asked Fabrice. One of Scout's brothers, Shadow, was a member of an underground kink club. He needed Shadow to get in as a guest. There was only one reason: Zeus.

Damn, Clay got goosebumps just thinking the guy's name. While Scout had definitely sidetracked him, he hadn't forgotten the pure lust of simply being in Zeus' company. He owned Affinity—the kink club they had visited that night. Clay was fully aware Zeus had been literally bred to use his sexiness to get close to anyone. All the Agafonov brothers, along with Zeus, had been born, raised, and trained in a Russian spy program. They each had a specific skill. Getting into anyone's bed for information or assassination was Zeus' forte. It didn't matter if a person knew that about him. Knowledge and brainpower had nothing to do with it. That beauty was built for sex, and it was impossible to ignore. Logically, Clay understood that Zeus kissing him wasn't personal. But that was all it had taken to toss Clay into a full-blown obsession, even though Clay had refused to let Zeus see he was moved. Clay had his pride and knew his limits. His heart didn't stand a single chance against that god. Not only did he not have that much game, but he had also always been a ragingly jealous person. All it would take was one night of Zeus working that club and Clay would become the next big serial killer. That was one thing he had learned as part of Beau's army: he could and would kill a man.

The sound of his cellphone ringing poured through the car speakers, startling Clay from his thoughts. Scout's name showed on the car's infotainment screen. Sometimes it was like Scout knew Clay thought about Zeus. He always saved Clay from heading down an idiotic road.

Clay hit the button on his steering wheel to answer. "Hello?"

"Where did you go?"

Just the sound of Scout's voice made him smile. "I had to get out of the house. There's a club on the beach called Hula Moon Club. I thought I'd check it out."

For a moment, only silence met his words. Clay almost apologized for leaving without saying anything. Scout spoke before Clay broke. "Sounds like fun. I'll meet you over there."

Clay shook his head at his own weaknesses. His smile was out of control, though. "Great. I'll see you there."

"Yep." With only that chirped word between them, Scout disconnected the call.

Metal music went back to blasting throughout the car. Clay dissociated for the rest of the drive. When he pulled into the overflowing parking lot, the only thing that stopped him from leaving was Scout being on his way. There was nowhere to park, and he was instantly nervous at the size of the crowd. As if God sent him a challenge, he had to slam on his brakes to keep from getting hit when a car unexpectedly backed from its parking spot. Clay couldn't be irritated. He slid in right behind the guy. Clay practically felt every car behind him raging at Clay for getting a decent space. He gathered his stuff and his courage and then stepped out.

An ocean breeze rushed over him, bringing with it the scent of tropical flowers and salt. Clay breathed in the smell. He loved it here. Every time they came, Clay dreamed about staying. No one left Beau, and he couldn't leave Fabrice behind, so Clay pushed the fantasy from his head. He probably wouldn't be happy here full time anyhow. In his heart, he knew what he loved was the feeling of being on vacation. If he lived here, eventually, he would want to get away from here too.

His thoughts carried him to paying the cover charge and diving into the crowd. The place was a tad different from what he expected. There were a lot more leather daddies than he had pictured. Clay went straight to the bar and ordered a beer. He swallowed half his drink before deciding to turn around and people-watch. His breath caught. Clay's vision zoomed in on the cut body headed his way. Even in the darkness mixed with neon lights, Clay felt the power of Scout's stare. Having Scout's attention was a little frightening. He saw everything: every flaw and shame.

Still, Scout didn't look at anyone else, even when people tried talking to him. He weaved through gyrating bodies until he stood toe to toe with Clay. As if that wasn't close enough, he boxed Clay in against the bar and leaned in to speak against Clay's ear.

"Just one question. Were you trying to escape me?"

God help him. Clay found himself clutching Scout's shirt. Even while holding the neck of his bottle, he managed to get some shirt with that hand too. He couldn't let Scout get away. "I knew you'd find me. You're probably tracking my phone."

A soft, sexy as fuck laugh brushed the shell of his ear. Scout reached between them and stole Clay's beer. As he watched Scout down his drink while still holding eye contact, Clay knew he was in trouble. He had Scout's undivided attention, and Clay was totally in.

Scout polished off Clay's beer and set the bottle aside. Free of that holding them back, Scout took Clay's hand and led him onto the dance floor. Clay looked nervous as hell. He kept chewing his bottom lip and breaking eye contact. Then his gaze would shoot back to holding Scout's stare, as if he refused to look like a coward. He knew. Scout saw that too. Clay knew Scout would be in his bed tonight. Like most friends, Clay wouldn't want to fuck up what they had.

He obviously hadn't realized that what they had was hardcore sexual attraction. It had always been inevitable that they would fuck. Scout had only been biding his time, waiting for the signs to move. Clay running away from him tonight turned out to be the trigger he needed pulled. He had waited too long, and that had sent Clay running. Scout couldn't allow that.

With Clay in his arms, Scout moved against him. He allowed no space between them. This was a club where people came to find a hookup for the night. Scout wanted no misunderstandings. Clay was his for the night.

Scout skimmed his lips across the shell of Clay's ear. There was no mistaking the chill bumps on his neck. Scout kissed those too, making things worse.

Clay's breathing turned faster. Yeah. He knew there was no going back.

"You're crossing a line we can't uncross."

Scout smiled against Clay's neck. "That line has never existed between us, and you know it."

"You should let me cut in." The booming voice broke the spell Scout tried to weave.

Clay immediately took a step back and motioned toward Scout, silently offering Scout to the man who had interrupted his plans. He wore a leather harness along with leather pants. Scout's gaze moved between the objectively sexy interloper to Clay and back again.

Scout shrugged. Maybe a hint of jealousy was exactly what Clay needed.

Scout smirked at his new dance partner and motioned him closer.

Lips immediately pressed against his ear to be heard over the noise surrounding them. "Jay."

"Scout." He didn't know why they exchanged names. Scout already knew who he would leave with tonight.

"You have a last name, Scout?"

Honestly, Scout was a tad annoyed. Clay hadn't gone back to the bar. He danced nearby, laughing with a blond.

"Agafonov." He didn't know why he had done that. Now would come the inevitable questions about his accent and surname.

"That's what I thought." The unmistakable feeling of a knife pressed against the spot beneath his ribs. "Move toward the back exit. Don't draw any attention, or you'll be dead in less than five seconds." There it was: the Russian accent. It was another operative. Scout had gotten complacent. Living with Beau had given him a sense of protection. He had let his guard down, and here he was. Scout danced his way toward the door Jay had indicated. He didn't draw attention to himself or look for Clay. The last thing Scout wanted was for Clay to get hurt because of him. Plus, Jay obviously underestimated Scout. Scout fought another smirk. This time, for a different reason. Jay didn't know him. He had been off the leash for over a decade. There were no rules for him.

Darkness engulfed them as Scout stepped outside. The alley where the club obviously dumped its trash was completely devoid of life. That was good, since Jay was about to lose his life right here. Scout readied himself while ensuring no move he made gave him away.

"I suggest you drop that knife if you want to keep your head."

Scout blinked. Clay stood behind Jay with a gun pressed against the back of Jay's head. Scout couldn't believe Clay got the drop on both of them.

The knife hit the ground.

Scout felt Jay tense, readying to attack. Before he could, Clay had Jay's arm at an odd angle with Jay bent and twisted with the gun still against the guy's head.

"Don't even think about it, motherfucker. You have no idea who you've fucked with."

Despite the pain Jay had to be in, Jay chuckled. "He no longer has our government backing him. You're the one fuck-ing with the wrong one."

An evil smile stretched Clay's lips.

Scout took a step back. This was a man Scout hadn't met.

"Oh, I didn't mean him. It's me you won't walk away from."

Goddamn. He was sexy.

Clay's gaze flickered his way. "Call Beau. Let him know we were attacked. We need a cleanup crew."

That got Jay's attention. He struggled against Clay's hold. If Clay even noticed, he didn't show it. Meanwhile, Scout was shocked into complete uselessness. Jay was trained by the same people as Scout and Clay treated him as if his skill was nonexistent, which enraged Jay more by the second. He spat, cursed, and fought.

Clay calmly held him twisted like a pretzel with one hand and a gun to the guy's head with the other.

All Scout could do was take out his phone and call Beau, as ordered. He imagined this was one for the private line.

Beau answered on the first ring, proving the number was only for emergencies. "What's happened?"

"We've been attacked."

"Is my boy hurt?" The bite to Beau's tone was even more terrifying than Clay's cold calm.

"Not yet. Threat hasn't been neutralized. Clay says we'll need a cleanup crew."

"Put me on speaker."

Scout didn't hesitate. "You're on."

"Are you hurt?"

"No, I'm good."

"That's my boy." Clay smirked. Beau continued while Scout couldn't look away from Clay. "You know where to put him. I'm on my way."

"Yes, sir."

"Can our new guest hear me?"

Clay's gaze flickered toward Jay, as if checking to see if he was still conscious—like the guy wasn't still struggling. "Yes, sir."

"Good. When I get there, you'll wish my boy had killed you. No one fucks with one of mine. Think on it while you wait for me. I bet you can't even dream of what I'll do to you. Your people know not to touch the Bosi family. It looks like they need reminding."

The phone disconnected, and Jay went limp, as if the fire bled from him. "No one mentioned anything about the Bosi family. I was instructed only to retrieve a defector."

Clay made a low humming sound. "Well, let this be lesson number one. Not asking questions gets you killed. Come on." He repositioned their bodies to hide the gun between them as he marched Jay to his car.

Scout hopped in the back. He wouldn't risk anything happening to Clay on the drive. "We'll come back for the other car tomorrow."

Clay tossed him a wink, and everything inside Scout sang. He would be absolute fire in bed. Jay should die twice just for that interruption alone. Scout had never been more primed.

Chapter Four

THE NIGHT TURNED OUT to be a hell
of a lot longer than Clay expected.
A week of preparations had to be
slashed to only hours. With their un-
willing guest locked away, Scout and
he rushed through the house doing all
the last-minute inspections. They had
scheduled the maid service for tomorrow. That left Scout and him with
the job of tossing bedding on top of
beds as quickly as possible. By the time
they were done, Scout looked exhausted. Clay couldn't stop tossing looks his
way, checking for any signs of his earlier ordeal. On his part, Clay was still

enraged. That fucking piece of shit had held a knife on Scout. Clay was ready to tear him apart. But orders were orders, and Beau—with the help of Henry, no doubt—wanted him alive. In the smallest of ways, Clay felt slightly bad for the guy. If Jay spoke the truth about only following orders, and Scout seemed to think that was the case, then Jay hadn't known how massive of a mistake he had made. His shitty leaders had sent him in blind to a situation he couldn't win. Jobs like these weren't personal. Clay would know. He had been there.

"What are you thinking so hard about? You have a very intense look going on over there."

Clay smiled at Scout's observation. "It's just been a hell of a night, and it's not over. Beau will be here soon."

"I'm sure he won't expect you to stay awake when he gets here."

Clay shrugged. "Honestly, I have no clue what will happen. It's been a while since I've heard Beau that angry."

They stood in the center of the main family room and held each other's stare. It was obvious neither of them knew what to say.

Scout stepped closer and rubbed Clay's arms, as if trying to warm him. "Don't stress too much about this. Beau is one calculating motherfucker. I doubt he'll actually walk into anything with nothing but blind rage."

Clay lifted one shoulder in a half shrug. "I don't even know why I'm worried about what he'll do."

The comforting expression Scout wore soothed Clay's frayed nerves. "Because you're a good person and you know that guy is just a puppet. But whoa, dude. That hold was impressive as hell. Jay isn't just some guy with a knife. He's a trained assassin. You acted as if he was nothing."

The complementary speech confused Clay a little. "I'm on Beau's security team."

A smile stretched Scout's lips. "You say that as if I should've realized you're a badass. In retrospect, I guess I should've. Not just anyone has what it takes to guard such a huge target. Of course, this has a thousand other questions running through my mind. Like how exactly were you trained? Is the entire army of guards trained the same?"

"They learn from me."

Scout jumped at Henry's appearance. Then he was shoved out of the way by Beau's massive right-hand man. "Are you okay?" He patted Clay as if searching for injuries.

"I'm o—"

Henry was shoved aside. Beau looked panicked. "Tell me what happened. Are you sure you're all right?"

A nervous chuckle escaped Clay. He wasn't used to being fussed over.

Scout jumped in and saved him. "You should've seen him. He was amazing. In seconds, he had everything under control without even breaking a sweat. It was awesome to behold."

Clay fought an uncomfortable smile. He wasn't good at handling praise.

Beau ignored him. "It was the longest flight of my life trying to get here." He ran a shaky hand over his eyes.

Clay couldn't stop studying his every reaction.

Beau's adorable husband, Kylo, stood at his side, hugging a teddy bear while rocking from one foot to the other, as if he too was a nervous wreck. "You really scared Daddy. He fretted the whole way here. You're like a son to him."

Beau already had his head together with Henry, discussing their next move.

Clay's gaze moved that way before jumping back to Kylo. "Thanks for that. He made sure I was prepared for exactly this. Everything is okay."

Kylo jumped forward and hugged him. "I'm happy you're safe too."

A genuine smile touched his lips. Kylo was a breath of fresh air.

Kylo took a step back. He squared his shoulders, taking on as hard of a look as he could considering it was him... and he wore a hot pink tutu with electric blue leggings. "Where is this bully? I want to get a hit in too." He hopped, shooting one arm toward an invisible opponent in what looked to be an acceptably good punch.

It took everything Clay possessed to not laugh. He didn't get a chance to respond.

Beau obviously heard the question. "You're not getting involved with this."

Kylo's bottom lip shot out.

Beau threw his hands up. "For fuck's sake. Come on, then."

Kylo bounced in place, wearing a huge grin.

Beau focused on Clay. "You should head to bed. I'm sure you're exhausted. Don't worry about work. You're on vacation."

Clay nodded. "Yes, sir."

Beau held his stare for longer than was necessarily comfortable. He cleared his throat. "I'm damn glad you're okay."

A smile exploded across Clay's face. "I love you too."

Henry chuckled.

Beau shook his head and walked away, but not before squeezing his shoulder. Most people never saw this side of Beau. All the kids he raised were major exceptions. Occasionally, he let his mask slip. Clay was damn glad for it.

Scout watched the entire exchange with two parts disbelief and one part jealousy. When Clay had told him the story of growing up in Beau's care, he hadn't formed any pictures to match that life. He just couldn't see Beau as a loving father, even though he had taken in all of Scout's family too. This was a side of Beau he never would have thought existed. Seeing behind his mask first-hand was a huge weight off his chest. He had wondered several times how long it would take before Beau no longer had use for them and made them disappear. He saw it now. Whether they did the odd job for him or not, Beau had opened his home to them, and everyone under his roof mattered to him in some fashion. Scout's gaze moved over Clay. Obviously, some were more important than others, but there was a human buried somewhere inside Beau. He had suspected as much since Kylo had married the guy. But Kylo had a screw or two loose, so they were probably more alike than not.

"Well, I guess there's nothing left to do for the night. We should head to bed."

Clay's words pulled Scout from his thoughts. He fought hard for a way to flirt and get back to what they shared on that dance floor. His mind lagged. Clay headed for the back hall toward the long line of bedrooms. Scout panicked, but he still didn't know what to say to keep Clay from slipping away.

At the mouth of the hallway, Clay paused and looked his way. "Are you coming, or were you just toying with me earlier?"

Scout's feet moved before his brain caught up. It was obvious his body had better sense than his brain. "I'm com-ing."

A smirk passed over Clay's lips. "That's the plan."

Clay turned away, and Scout's knees weakened. The door to the confidence Clay hid had been kicked open tonight. It seemed Clay had chosen to stay in beast mode for a little longer. Scout adjusted the bulge in his jeans that kept growing on the way to Clay's room. One thing Scout had noticed about Clay right away was his amazing ass. Now he couldn't look away from that masterpiece. Fuck.

His lust was off the charts. He couldn't take another second of the hunger. In one long stride, Scout had one hand around Clay's jaw and the other tearing open the front of Clay's pants. While molded against Clay's back, Scout dove inside Clay's underwear and roughly palmed Clay's cock. He sucked Clay's neck while Clay openly moaned. Anyone could catch them at any second. Scout couldn't stop. He ground his lower body against the perfect ass that had broken him. Scout needed Clay's screams. He wanted his cum. He couldn't wait another second to have what Clay had teased him with for months.

"Bedroom," Clay choked out between harsh breaths.

"Right here." Scout sounded almost inhuman with the growl in his voice. He couldn't help it. Clay had done something to his head. "Blow for me right here where anyone could watch." He bit Clay's ear, making Clay gasp. "Give me that cum." He tugged ruthlessly, leaving Clay with no other choice but to gasp and writhe in his hold. The satisfaction that roiled through him when a tiny cry reverberated from the hallway's walls and Clay jerked in his hold was like nothing else he had ever experienced. He stroked until he stole every twitch before he released Clay.

Scout brought his hand to his mouth and licked the cum from his fingers. "Now we can go." Even he was terrified of how possessive he felt in that moment. Clay was his.

Clay's entire body shook as he stumbled into his bedroom. He didn't have time to catch his breath. Scout kicked the door closed behind them and was on him. The tongues clashed. Scout tore at Clay's clothes. He could barely breathe from how fast his heart raced. Scout had already pulled an orgasm from him, and Clay already wanted more. Clay's cum still lingered on Scout's tongue from him licking his fingers clean. Goddamn. That had been one of the sexiest things he had ever seen. One second, they were in the hallway under the threat of getting caught. The next thing he knew, Clay was on his back with a sexy as fuck guy who acted crazed to have him. The entire experience was a huge ego boost and a mind-fuck. No one made him feel as much as Scout did. Never in his life had he felt more desired. He wanted to fuck.

"Tell me where to look."

Clay didn't know how he knew what Scout meant. It was like they were in each other's heads. "Toiletries bag. It's on the bathroom counter."

Scout pushed from the bed and headed for the bathroom, peeling his shirt off as he went. Clay's mind went hazy. His vision narrowed to a pinpoint. Scout's body was gorgeous. He made Clay weak as hell.

"When I get back, the rest of those clothes better be gone."

Clay considered toying with him, asking what Scout would do if he didn't comply.

He was out of his clothes too fast to take the passing thought seriously.

Scout returned. The button on his jeans was undone and his zipper down. His hips moved with the confidence of a man who knew his worth. Clay couldn't look away.

Scout climbed onto the bed and straddled Clay's body. "I have questions."

The switch from desperation to calm had a nervous laugh burbling in Clay's throat. "I maybe have answers."

"Are you gay?"

That uncomfortable chortle showed itself. "A dude just gave me a handjob and is currently straddling my nude body. That seems like an unnecessary question at this point."

Scout stared down at him, looking completely serious. "You have condoms but no lube."

Oh, boy. He found all the discomfort. Another nervous laugh escaped him. "Technically, I'm bi. Truthfully, I don't even know if those condoms are in date. I haven't touched anyone in like three years."

If Scout had any thoughts on Clay's confession, he didn't show it. He tossed the condom aside and lowered himself until he could swipe lips with Clay.

Clay's eyes fell closed. He didn't know what went on inside Scout's head, but he got the feeling sex just got taken off the table. It was times like these that reminded Clay why he had turned his back on men. Nothing he ever did was right. He was too inexperienced or too needy. Clay expected too much or played things too cool. No matter what he gave, it wasn't enough.

Frustration rose in his throat, choking him. He turned his face away. "You don't have to let me down easy, or whatever this is. You're free to leave."

Scout bit his ear, tearing a gasp of surprise from Clay. He immediately kissed the spot he had bitten. "This isn't me stopping. I'm slowing down. You deserve more attention than I've given you."

His muscles relaxed a hair. His thoughts swung wildly. He wanted all the time he could get with Scout, but he also didn't want to be known as the guy who needed easing into things. They had started this wild and hot in the hall-

way. Clay would finish their night together the same way.

"You can do that later." Clay used all
the skills in his arsenal to have Scout
flipped on his back and under him in
a flash. He didn't give Scout a chance
to clear his head. He was down Scout's
body and sucking his dick with zero
chill in under thirty seconds.

Scout's hips left the bed. His fingers
dove into Clay's hair. "Oh, fuck."

A sense of wickedness overcame Clay.
He could make Scout curse all night.
This was very likely a one-night thing.
Scout didn't strike him as the serious
type. Clay couldn't think about that
right now. He was a needy bitch. It
would hurt like hell when Scout pretended nothing had happened.

Clay bobbed on Scout's cock. Saliva ran down his hands. He had jumped on Scout's dick too quickly to completely undress him. Clay worked to peel off Scout's pants and underwear without letting Scout get distracted. He loved the way Scout fucked his mouth a little too much. Once he had Scout's jeans on the floor, Clay really settled in. He swirled his tongue around Scout's crown while using his saliva-coated fingers to toy with Scout's asshole. Scout didn't protest. Clay fingered him.

"Holy hell, dude. Oh, my God."

Clay wanted to pat himself on the back, but his hands were busy.

Scout babbled curse words and praise. The sound of Scout's lust-filled voice had him on edge. He moved against the mattress, trying to get relief. His mind and body were pulled in too many directions at once. It shocked the hell out of him when cum hit the back of throat. He nearly gagged in his surprise. But Clay fully took advantage of freeing one hand. He tugged and pulled his dick. An orgasm was already so close, he could taste it. He blew in less than five strokes while still licking Scout clean. When Clay felt confident he had gotten the job done, he crawled up the bed and collapsed next to Scout, sounding like he had run a marathon. He couldn't catch his breath. Clay stared at the ceiling and gasped. But then he turned his head, and so did Scout. Their gazes met. They burst into laughter. Clay had no clue what was so funny. Yet he couldn't control the wheezing guffaws leaving him. He was just so fucking happy.

"Ahhh," Scout sighed, getting himself under control first. He rolled Clay's way and straddled him. "Now that's what I call friendship." Even as Scout kissed him, part of Clay shriveled. There it was. At least Scout hadn't kept him guessing. This encounter meant nothing. Clay supposed he was used to that.

Chapter Five

FOR A GOOD HALF an hour, Clay stared at Scout's sleeping form. It surprised the hell out of him to wake up and find Scout still there. It took less than ten minutes for Clay to realize he wallowed in the hell he had created. He had gone into things with his eyes wide open. Clay had known this would lead to nothing more than possibly friends with benefits. The problem was, as much as he had wanted last night, he didn't want this morning. Clay had been searching for something real for a while now. He had to back away from this before he got hurt. They lived under the same roof. He had already made that mistake. Clay already pretended not to care about things that murdered his soul a little more every day. He had to stop digging.

As quietly as possible, Clay slipped from the bed and shut himself away in the bathroom. He brushed his teeth and avoided his reflection while the shower heated up. The water in this place took forever to get warm. It was annoying. By the time Clay stepped beneath the water, he was irritated in a way he couldn't explain. Everything pissed him off. He wanted to punch someone.

The shower door opened, and a nude Scout stood in the opening. Their gazes met. Clay snapped. He hauled Scout inside and shoved him against the wall. Their kiss was explosive, bordering on violent. He palmed their dicks, holding them together as he stroked. The pressure wasn't enough. He wanted more, but he was also too enraged to slow down enough to try a different approach.

Scout's nails dug into Clay's shoulders.

Clay wanted it. He needed to hurt on the outside so he could forget the way this killed him on the inside. Clay wasn't this guy. He was relationship material. Clay honestly believed that. No one wanted anything real any longer, and Clay didn't even know who to lash out at.

Scout pulled away from their kiss. "Take a breath." He kissed Clay's neck. "I'm not going anywhere. We have time."

Clay took a breath. Scout was right. He had pulled Scout into this shower. It wasn't like Scout had forced his way in. He wasn't being fair by taking his frustration out on Scout. Clay did this to himself. He forced himself to slow. When the tension left his shoulders, his hips rolled. This time, Scout initiated their kiss, and it was sweet as hell. While the passion hadn't lessened, this kiss felt more personal. His eyes stung. He felt special to Scout, and that was a knife to his chest. But Clay couldn't stop because he was starved as hell for affection. He lapped up the loving way they touched like a man dying of thirst. His mind played tricks on him. The same dumbassery that had led to him spending every night praying Fabrice would love Clay the way Clay had always loved him stirred inside him. It was crazy to expect Scout to jump right into a full-blown relationship with him. Of course, he needed time. Clay just needed to relax. Go slower. He was okay.

Scout dropped his forehead, resting it on Clay's shoulder. "Damn, Clay. You have no idea how badly I want you inside me. Tonight, we stay in my room."

Happiness flared to life inside him. Scout sounded like he wasn't done. "You won't regret me." With that promise hanging between them, Clay worked harder to please Scout. He needed to feel Scout blow in his hand. There were so many ways Clay wanted to fuck him. He could keep Scout high. Unfortunately, everything he did to Scout happened to him as well. He sucked air, doing his best to hold on. Scout's dick felt way too good against his. He clenched his stomach muscles.

Scout cried out. Cum shot from him while Scout whined his way through his orgasm. Clay snagged Scout's chin and forced his head against the wall, holding him there. It took Clay a few strokes more before he joined Scout over the edge. As pulses of pleasure stole his soul, Clay's gaze never wavered from staring at Scout. He knew exactly who got him so fucking hot, and his eyes refused to look away—like watching porn. Scout was in his head. Truthfully, he had no clue how it happened.

Scout headed for the kitchen. He needed fortification. Clay had gone in search of Henry to get the lowdown on the Jay business. The delicious scent of all the perfect breakfast foods filled the dining room. To his surprise, Fabrice was setting up a mound of plates at the table.

He glanced up as Scout stepped into the room. "Hey. You're the first person I've seen this morning. I guess everyone had a late night."

Scout pasted on a bright smile. He didn't have to fake it. Clay had made his entire goddamn morning. "Hey. When did you get into town?" He pulled out a chair and sat.

Fabrice glanced at his watch. "About three hours ago. With Beau and Kylo coming in early, some of us needed to rush here as well. Sorry your peace was disturbed early. You probably enjoyed the time alone since it's always hopping back home."

"I wasn't alone," Scout said absently as he filled his plate.

Silence fell between them. Scout focused on his task. It took a second for Scout to realize it wasn't a comfortable one. He met Fabrice's stare again. The chef's expression was completely closed. His gaze dropped a hair to Scout's neck before he went back to arranging plates. "I see."

Scout had no fucking clue what that was about.

An obnoxious squeal rent the air, jerking Scout's attention away. Clay skipped through the doorway and tried climbing Fabrice like a jungle gym. "It's my friend!" He kissed Fabrice loudly on the cheek while Fabrice smiled like an idiot and swiped at his face.

A spew of French spilled from Fabrice.

Clay laughed and backed away. "Please spare me. You know you love me. Quit threatening to put me in timeout. You'd get bored without me."

Scout's gaze moved between the two. A bad feeling scratched at his gut. They had known each other their whole lives. There was a very good chance they had been more than friends at some point. Scout thought he had gotten past this feeling of something being between the two. Now he saw them together again, and the ugly sensation in his gut was back.

Clay grabbed a chair and pulled it close to Scout. He stole a piece of Scout's bacon. "Awww. You fixed me a plate."

Scout slapped his hand away. "Mine, lazy ass. There's a whole table of food."

Clay's eyes swam with laughter as he ate his nefariously gained treat. "Did you know you have a hickey?"

That explained Fabrice's judge-y look. "I didn't, but whose fault is that?"

Fabrice walked away without unloading his entire cart onto the table.

An alarm rang in the back of Scout's mind. He wouldn't stew. "Did we do something wrong?"

Clay stood and took care of the work Fabrice had left behind. He shrugged. "Who knows? I imagine he's just busy.

Timing is everything when serving a huge household."

Scout eyed Clay. He genuinely looked un-concerned and/or clueless. As long as any longing wasn't reciprocated with Fabrice, Scout wouldn't worry. It was Scout's bed Clay intended to share tonight.

Clay glanced toward the kitchen. A deep line appeared between his eyes. "I'll check on him, just in case." Clay headed inside the kitchen.

Like a crazy person, Scout shifted his chair trying to catch a glimpse of the pair inside. With the way the area was designed, he couldn't see a thing. As the minutes passed by, Scout's jealousy grew.

Before he decided to make an ass of himself, Clay reappeared. He didn't look any less concerned than when he left. Clay reclaimed his seat. His gaze locked on Scout. Scout immediately knew he wouldn't like whatever Clay said next. He was right. "Is it okay if I take a raincheck on tonight? Fabrice wants me to spend some time with him. I guess he has some sort of drama going on, and I'm his best friend, so..."

Scout ground his back teeth but somehow hid his rage. "You're on best-friend duty. I get it." He really did. Fabrice had seen Clay slipping away and realized he couldn't wait any longer to make his move. What an asshole. He'd had nearly their entire lives and now he hoped to steal Clay from Scout. Clay might be blind to Fabrice, but Scout saw him.

Scout wouldn't be thwarted that easily. "Come to my bed anyhow. I don't care how late it is. I'll be waiting."

"Are you sure? I don't want to disturb your sleep."

Scout managed to pull out a wicked smile. His gaze raked down Clay's body before meeting his stare again. "Positive."

Clay fidgeted a little, looking nervous. "Okay." He was such a conundrum. Shy one second and badass the next. "Are you really okay with me hanging out with Fabrice tonight? I'm opening the line of clear communication you asked for here."

Yeah. Scout wasn't about to fuck up this budding thing by telling Clay he couldn't spend time with his best friend.

He forced an overly bright smile. "Of course. I'm not your boyfriend. You can do whatever you want."

Something flickered across Clay's features. Whatever thought he had at Scout's statement, Clay hid it too fast for Scout to read him. "Yeah. Okay. I hear you." He glanced around as if looking for an escape.

A pit grew in Scout's stomach. They were going backwards, and he didn't know how to stop.

Clay slapped his knees and stood. "Well, Fabrice is way behind on today's prep since he came in so late and hasn't been to bed yet. I'm going to take over for the next few hours so he can get some sleep." A fake-looking smile appeared on his lips. "Plus, with him gone, I can steal all the good stuff he keeps hidden in the kitchen."

A genuine snort burst from Scout at the mischievousness in Clay's expression. "Have fun. I need to hit the security room and get ready for Tracker. My guess is they have him coming in early too."

Clay nodded. "Sounds good." He bent and stole a kiss. It was way too quick. Clay looked slightly mortified when he pulled away. "Sorry. I guess I need to control myself. It's way too easy to forget where the line begins and ends with you."

Scout had no fucking clue what that meant, so he said nothing.

Clay smiled, but it looked sad. "Have a good day. I'll see you... whenever, I guess." He headed for the kitchen, practically scrambling away from Scout. Scout stared after him with his heart in his throat. What in the fuck was he supposed to do now?

Chapter Six

A WARM NIGHT BREEZE ruffled Clay's hair as he sat at the edge of the pool, dangling his legs in the water. Hawaii was so goddamn beautiful, and he let himself dream again that he could live here full time. He might be trained every bit as well as any other Bosi guard, but Clay didn't truly have a fighter's soul. Everything inside him craved quiet, peaceful beauty. A life of violence had been given to him. Clay never would've chosen his path.

A shadow grew bigger on the water.

Clay smiled. Fabrice might be a calm, soothing person, but Clay always felt him when he was near. His presence was too familiar to Clay for him to hide.

Fabrice filled the space beside him and put his bare feet in the water. Hip to hip, they sat in silence. Clay didn't know what Fabrice had going on, but he could be here.

"I forgot to ask what happened to that guy who brought Beau scrambling here."

Clay leaned his shoulder against Fabrice, soaking up the only real connection he had in the world. "In one of the world's craziest 'it's a small world' stories, it turns out the guy had stopped once to help Kylo change a flat tire like three years ago. I guess he was probably in town, stalking the Agafonov brothers. It was just one of those random-ass things." Clay shrugged. "Or maybe he had been meant to meet Kylo and have his life spared now. You know how life can be funny like that. Beau took out his kneecaps and sent him home to Russia as a failure. From what Henry tells me, they'll either kill him for failing his mission or they'll dump him in some freezing back alley to die from his injuries and the elements. Either way, Jay gets a horrible death, and Beau can still say he didn't kill the guy."

Fabrice blew out a soft sigh. "Well, that's a new leaf for Beau. You really should have seen him. We've seen him in some deeply dark places over the years, and this was still epic—like the kind of explosive rage he flew into when Boone tried to kill himself."

Clay shook his head. He couldn't believe that. Boone was Beau's oldest son. When he had nearly succeeded at taking his own life several years ago, Beau had been inconsolable, and his temper had sent them all into hiding. Clay couldn't see Beau being the same for him.

"Can't picture it."

A soft chuckle rumbled from Fabrice. He turned his head and kissed Clay's forehead. "You've always been too blind to realize how much people care about you."

Clay wanted to laugh off the words, but they cut too close to the bone. He had never been good at spotting love. The only person he knew who loved him for real was Fabrice.

Fabrice cleared his throat. "So, Scout, huh?"

Truthfully, Clay didn't want to answer that. He would end up looking like a fool all over again when Scout found his person. Clay didn't speak. He knew—in itself—silence was an answer. But he couldn't open his mouth and have happiness fall out when he knew Scout only wanted to be friends. Scout had reiterated that point at breakfast.

Fabrice blew out a slow sigh. "I suppose I should've seen that one coming. When he kissed you at Affinity, I was standing there. But you hadn't really said anything else about it, and I thought you had a crush on Zeus."

Clay smiled. "You just made me sound like I'm twelve."

Fabrice's mouth lifted in one corner. The half-smile fell away as quickly as it appeared. "I thought you wanted quiet freedom. You have a better shot at that with Zeus. With Scout, you'll be trapped with the family forever. Beau might actually let you move on to a happy life if you're with someone powerful and connected to the family. Zeus could save you."

Every word was like a punch to the chest. They knew each other too well. Something about everything Fabrice said hurt his heart. "I hear you, but you missed a key detail: Zeus doesn't want me. That guy doesn't want anyone. Not really." Clay's gaze moved to the gorgeous tropical trees and flowers surrounding the pool. He felt like he was in a hidden paradise. Clay needed a balm on his soul before he finished his thought. "No one really wants me."

Silence met his claim.

Clay turned his head and found Fabrice staring at him with fire dancing in his eyes. "That's not true, and you know it."

Here they were again. Clay desperately wished he had never acted on a moment of weakness and kissed Fabrice, stepping over an invisible line two years ago. Now all either of them did was act like nothing changed and do every act of friendship as over-the-top as possible. It was as if they fought to convince each other of some lie.

This time, Clay couldn't back away from this conversation. "You're the one who said you didn't want us. You're the one who said everyone would flip out since we had been raised like brothers. Please don't look at me like I'm killing you. I already had to mourn you."

Fabrice looked away. "Never mind. Forget I said anything. You're a grown man. Get your heart broken. Lose your chance to get away. What do I care?" Fabrice stood and headed for the house.

A growl of frustration rose in Clay's throat. "Fabrice." He couldn't stop himself from calling out.

Fabrice turned. He looked closed—like he had withdrawn all care from Clay.

Clay's shoulders sagged. All he ever did was somehow end up alone. "I heard what you said. You know I love you and value your opinion. I'll keep every word you said in mind. You know I can't take you being mad at me."

Fabrice seemed to deflate. He dropped his defensive stance and moved back to Clay. Fabrice bent and kissed Clay's forehead again. "I'm not mad at you, beautiful. I'm mad at myself. Just be happy, okay?"

Clay nodded. His throat tightened. He wanted to tell his best friend that he didn't know how to find joy in anything. But Clay had a bad feeling Fabrice wasn't his best friend any longer and hadn't been for a while. Like everything else, that was on him. Clay might have no choice about living with Fabrice, but he could stop making things worse by showing up. It was like ripping out his own heart, but Fabrice would be better off without him in his life.

Red and black makeup ran down the drain. Thankfully, Scout had gotten good at washing off the clown face in record time. Anytime he had to get too close to a target, Scout chose a clown persona. Not only did the move hide his identity, but clowns made people un-comfortable. Nothing could make peo-ple cross the street and not look directly at someone like an evil-looking harle-quin. It was harder for a witness to pick him out of a lineup if they refused to look at him.

While technically Scout hadn't left the Bosi estate, he didn't take chances. If anyone saw him, he might draw too much attention to the property. He would never jeopardize the family just to soothe his jealousy. Unfortunately, eavesdropping only left him with more questions than answers. He had heard every word said between Fabrice and Clay. He wished he hadn't caught the part about Scout keeping him tied to a family Clay seemingly wanted to leave behind. Clay had never acted anything other than happy with the people in his life. Now he knew Clay wanted something more than this life, and he couldn't unlearn that.

With his face clean, Scout tossed his shirt and towel into the laundry chute before stepping out into his bedroom. Clay sat on the edge of the bed, waiting. Emotions overwhelmed him, the way they always did when he saw Clay. His gorgeous hazel eyes always stole Scout's breath. His blond hair was a windblown mess. Scout would find a way to make sure Clay got the life he wanted, even if that meant Scout didn't get to keep him.

"Hey. I didn't think I'd see you for a while."

Clay smirked. "I can't tell if you're a terrible liar or not. But I know you had to know I was on my way, since you sat in the bushes watching me all night."

Damn. That looked bad. He climbed onto the bed and settled on his back. Scout didn't want to look Clay in the eye and lie again. "I was worried about you. Fabrice is your best friend, but he's in love with you. I didn't know what would happen tonight. Jealousy is a hell of a motivator." Okay, so maybe he didn't intend to lie as boldly as he thought.

Clay's shoulders expanded like he drew an overly deep breath. "You don't want to hear anything about all that." Clay never looked Scout's way as he made the claim.

Scout brushed the tips of his fingers down the small of Clay's back. "You can talk to me about it. I'm your friend too."

Clay shot to his feet and tore off his shirt. "Yeah, I know. You've made it abundantly clear we're friends. I get it."

Scout blinked at the unexpected rage. Before he could figure out what just happened, Clay crawled onto the bed and straddled Scout. His tongue was in Scout's mouth before Scout could think of a single thing to say. Then, there were no thoughts. There was only Clay. Clay's kiss was almost punishing. All Scout could focus on was Clay shoving his shorts down his hips—like he planned to take what he wanted. Scout kind of wanted to slow things down and make sure Clay was good. Clay made any hesitation impossible. Scout was on fire. Nothing existed beyond the body covering him. Clay always made him feel like no one else existed. He had Clay's full attention, and Clay acted like there was nothing he wanted as desperately as he wanted to fuck Scout. Everything about Clay was a fucking ego trip. Scout couldn't quit him even if Clay chose someone else. He was an addict. Scout would follow Clay to the ends of the earth, tweaking for one more night.

Scout tore his mouth away. "Goddamn. Please fuck me already."

A wicked-sounding chuckle caressed his ears. "Tell me where."

Scout didn't play games. It was like they shared a brain right then. He pointed toward the nightstand. Scout had set everything they needed there earlier. He had known they would be impatient. It was like they were incapable of moving slowly.

Clay moved to his feet and stripped.

Scout watched with his heart in his throat. While Clay gave off no-game energy, the truth was he wasn't scared of shit. He had them nude in under two minutes. Clay gave him a whole-ass show while Scout watched. He rolled a condom down his length and coated the outside with lube. Clay didn't stop there. He climbed back onto the bed and between Scout's thighs. All Scout could do was enjoy the moment. Then Clay toyed with Scout's asshole. Scout forgot his own name. Everything disappeared but the sensation of Clay fingering him and stretching him. While Clay was a self-proclaimed bisexual, he obviously had his share of experience with men. Scout wasn't sure he would ever breathe properly again.

"Don't be afraid to critique me. I want to make you happy."

Clay hit that sweet spot as he made the claim, and Scout's hips left the bed. "Goddamn, Clay. You're doing great."

Clay's expression stayed closed. Scout had no clue how Clay felt. Honestly, his expressionless face was a bit unnerving. It was almost as if Clay wasn't there. His mind had gone elsewhere while his body ran on autopilot. Scout forgot to worry when Clay began slowly pressing his way in. His cock stretched

Scout, making Scout feel fuller than he ever had before. He loved it. Scout wanted it.

He ground his back teeth, desperately clinging to his patience. Scout recognized Clay tried not to hurt him. He couldn't take it any longer. "Fuck me." Even to Scout's ears, he sounded needy as fuck.

For a moment, they held each other's stare. Clay's lips were swollen from their violent kiss, and his cheeks were red. Then Clay slammed inside him, going as deeply as possible. Scout couldn't even blink. He couldn't look away from the way Clay's lips parted, and he turned even sexier with lust etching his features. Clay held his stare and rolled his hips, taking Scout at the perfect angle. Scout was so enthralled, he didn't look away or move. He just took it and lived the experience. Sex with Clay was hands down the hottest encounter he had ever had. Scout wanted to record every detail. He was probably the lousiest fuck Clay ever enjoyed. Scout was frozen with awe and all the goddamn emotions choking him.

He wanted time to stop. Scout had found what he craved having for the rest of his life, and Clay wasn't his. It seemed there should be something he could say to convince Clay to keep him. Unfortunately, all his tongue knew was cries and moans. Clay was so fucking intense, he didn't know if he would risk speaking even if he could. Scout wasn't sure if Clay would rather fight him instead. There was so much rage in every thrust, but—somehow—the entire experience was beautiful. The pleasure won.

It always did. The way his balls tightened and pressure climbed his erection wouldn't be ignored.

"Don't hold back."

At Clay's demand, Scout turned into the obedient piece of ass. He saw fucking stars as cum shot through the air. His cries bounced off the walls and were probably heard at the opposite end of the house. On the other side of the spectrum, Clay never made a sound. His motions quickened and then slowed before Clay kissed Scout like a starved man. Eventually, the thrusts stopped. Sweat and hard breathing ruled the moment. Scout floated in the clouds.

Intrusive thoughts hit. It was very possible that wasn't the best experience for Clay. He didn't know how to broach the topic, so he didn't say anything. Since

Clay kept giving him sweet kisses, Scout told himself everything was okay. Clay hadn't grabbed his clothes and ran.

He couldn't take it. "Next time, when I know to expect this level of phenomenal sex, I'll be better."

Clay chuckled and kissed Scout's neck. "You're thinking too much. That's my job. I have no complaints." His hand slid down Scout's side. "I'm happy to hear you want a next time."

Damn, Clay worried Scout wouldn't want him again? Was he insane? "Why do I get the feeling no one has ever told you, you're worth every second of their time? Because you're worth every second of mine."

Clay didn't respond. He simply continued kissing Scout's neck. Scout swore he felt Clay's unhappiness like a weight on his chest. It was a third person in the room. While Scout had no idea what went on in Clay's head, he knew he could make it better. Somehow, he would.

Chapter Seven

THEY WENT TO BREAKFAST. Scout hadn't realized such a small thing could feel so personal. Every new discovery with Clay made him want another. He had never been more terrified of becoming an addict. Truthfully, everything about Clay scared the shit out of him. They stared at their menus as if they were equally afraid to talk. Scout hated serious discussions. For his entire life, Scout had been forced to keep a tight lid on any emotions. Feelings were a weakness to be cut from them. The things they had to do required a cold detachment that was unbreakable. They couldn't come home after murdering other human beings and feel what they had done. Their minds would never survive it. Maybe Scout's mind hadn't lived on beyond his childhood. Scout felt things. He felt them deeply. But Scout wasn't good at expressing himself. As much as he hated when other people didn't communicate properly, when it came to emotions, he wasn't very good at putting his thoughts into words. It was a huge failing of his, actually. He would probably be a terrible boyfriend. As badly as he wanted to keep Clay to himself, he wasn't sure how to go about that or even if he could doom Clay to what would likely be a daily exercise in frustration for him.

Scout's gaze lifted from the menu. He caught Clay staring. Clay smirked. But-terflies stirred in Scout's stomach. Clay knew he could rock Scout's world. Scout knew it too, and it fucked with him hard.

"Hey. I didn't expect to find you here."

A large guy with perfectly styled hair and laughing brown eyes appeared at the edge of their table.

A smile lit Clay's face. "Jett. Hey. When did you make it to town?" Clay slid over in the booth as he questioned the new arrival... as if he knew this Jett guy a little too well.

Jett filled the empty space Clay made for him. "Late last night. I chose the last flight so I could make sure the house was good before leaving. You know me." His gaze slid Scout's way. "Who are you?" It couldn't have been more obvious Jett was in the long line of men crushing on Clay. He sounded exactly like he needed to know his competition.

Clay nodded Scout's way. "This is Scout. He's one of the Agafonov brothers." Clay motioned Jett's way. "This is Jett. He's a perimeter guard and doesn't live on property."

Jett eyed Scout. "What's your specialty?"

Scout held Jett's stare, letting him see the ruthless killer inside. "I shoot fast, accurate, and don't mind getting close and making it personal." Clay was his. Jett needed to recognize his place and stay there.

Clay jumped in, massaging his clavicle as he spoke, as if hurting. Oops. Scout had done that. "You should see him. He's fucking amazing. I've never seen anything like it. Scout can hit the dead center of a dozen targets, on the move, faster than you can see it happen. He's been trying to teach me, but I'm realizing it's probably a skill best learned from childhood. My vision and reflexes can't keep up or sync the way they should to do what he does."

Scout couldn't tear his gaze away from Clay throughout the entire speech. Clay looked and sounded as if Scout truly impressed him—like he was proud of Scout. Scout's chest warmed. His throat felt kind of funny. He was like moved and shit. No one had ever bragged about him in that way before.

Jett glanced between them.

Scout saw the battle brewing inside Jett between losing hope or doubling his efforts. He had no clue which choice Jett made because he changed tactics.

Jett focused on him, turning friendlier. "I met a few of your brothers on the flight last night. Tracker, Shadow, Ridge, and Zeus."

"Zeus isn't my brother."

Clay spoke over him. "Zeus is here?"

For fuck's sake. How many men on this trip would Scout have to wade his way through to keep Clay's attention? God-damn. He was exhausted just thinking about it.

Jett focused on Clay and nodded. "Yeah. From what I gathered, he's working on some project with Tracker. So he decided to tag along and help Tracker get the house here up to the same level of security as back home. In their downtime, they plan to put together some type of database. They didn't give details, and I didn't ask."

Scout fought the urge to massage his temples. He truly hoped Tracker kept Zeus out of sight and mind. As far as Scout was concerned, Zeus was his only true competition. Clay didn't look at anyone else the way he did Scout and Zeus. He honestly didn't know which Clay would choose if given a real ultimatum. Zeus would never want anything serious. In fact, a one-night stand was likely all anyone would get from that guy. Unfortunately, Scout didn't think he had much to offer someone as amazing as Clay, in the long run. What the fuck did he know about long-term relationships? Scout wasn't sure if he could even be considered fully human. The more Scout thought about the situation he had gotten himself into, the darker his mood became. Then Clay's foot brushed his beneath the table. Their gazes met and held. A weight lifted from Scout's chest, allowing him to breathe. Happiness and a deep longing filled him. Somehow, he would convince Clay to be with only him. No matter what it took.

Breakfast had been interesting. While Scout had been the one to suggest going out, he had acted strange, and Clay couldn't stop overthinking it. Before Jett interrupted, a few heated looks had passed between them. Afterward, Scout turned quiet. Their breakfast together went from feeling like a date to eating with a couple of friends. Clay fucking hated that. Every time he thought Scout showed signs of wanting more, Scout snatched his hope away.

Now, Clay shot moving targets in a sequestered bunker behind the vacation home. Scout gave pointers. Clay listened and tried to forget about last night. *Last night.* Holy shit. That had been the hottest night of Clay's entire life. Scout had acted so freaking needy. Clay didn't think Scout had been pretending. The begging had been in his eyes. Clay hadn't wanted to look away. He still fought the urge to stare into Scout's eyes and search for Scout's feelings.

"Let's do this."

Clay didn't have time to decipher Scout's words.

Scout pressed against his back, molding against him. He held Clay's wrist, guiding it to a certain target. "Take a breath." Scout kept him trained on the same target. "As I move from target to target, just follow your instincts and pull the trigger. You're overthinking each shot. Thinking slows your reaction time. You've handled weapons for a long time. You know when to shoot." Scout said each word against the shell of Clay's ear. Clay was hard as steel. Scout just aroused the fuck out of him.

"Now."

Clay pulled the trigger each time Scout pointed him toward a target. After a few seconds, he felt the moment he should fire. There was the slightest hint of hesitation. Scout didn't pause for even a full second. But Clay was so attuned to everything about him in that moment, he didn't miss a single thing about the way Scout held him. The magazine emptied. Clay hit the release, and Scout slapped in another. Clay recognized the pattern. He felt invincible. By the time the final magazine was empty, each breath Clay took heaved in and out. He sounded as if he had run a mile. Clay was ready to fuck.

Scout backed away, seemingly oblivious to the carnage he had caused. "You did amazing." Scout moved to the wall and hit the button to stop the targets. Once they settled, Scout removed each target and brought it to Clay for him to inspect. Each one was marked with a number.

Scout wore a huge grin. "Look at this."
He got close again, teasing Clay with his
heat. "You started on target three." He
motioned toward two of the bullet holes.
"These were already there. You can ignore those." He pointed out three more
and went in order of when they were
shot. "This is the first one." He moved
on to the next. "Second shot." He moved
to the third that was dead center. "This
is when my method clicked with you."
He waved a circle around the target.
"Notice these five are the only holes. You
shot this individual target eight times."

Clay was thoroughly distracted. "Did I
miss the other three times?" There was
a nervous chuckle with the question.
Maybe he hadn't been as tuned in as he
thought.

Scout smiled. "No. You hit the center perfectly each time. That's why this hole is slightly larger than the rest."

Clay blinked at the target. "Really?" Truthfully, he was more impressed with Scout than with himself. Clay already knew he couldn't make those shots again alone. "I can't believe how much you saw. You knew the exact target we started with and what order each target was hit down to the bullet placement. That's fucking amazing."

One side of Scout's mouth lifted in a sardonic smile. "We're talking about you. You were impressive as hell. We haven't even worked on rapid magazine exchange. You just automatically did it—like a pro."

They held each other's stare. Something passed between them. Clay felt Scout's intention to kiss him before Scout made a move. Before their lips met, the door swung open, blasting sunlight into the small building. Scout practically flew three feet backward. Clay didn't look toward the door right away. He wondered how much hurt showed in his expression before he hid behind a mask. Not that it mattered. Scout didn't look Clay's way. He focused on the door.

"Tracker. Hey... and Zeus."

At the mention of Zeus' name, Clay's gaze shot to the doorway. Tracker was distracted talking to Scout. Zeus' intense, permanently seductive stare was locked on Clay. Clay watched as Zeus walked toward him. Even the way he put one foot in front of the other was such an obviously practiced move that it had become a habit. It was like Scout saw Zeus for the first time. The real Zeus. It was like decoding Scout's training gave him the ability to decipher Zeus's as well. Everything about him was fake. His perfect smile meant nothing. Zeus didn't mean a damn thing he did.

"Hey."

Clay snapped out of his depressing discovery when Zeus spoke. His voice didn't match his false persona. There was a hint of genuine happiness in Zeus' greeting. When Clay returned Zeus' smile, it was real. "Hey. I didn't know you were coming on this trip." Clay knew Zeus was there thanks to Jett. But it was a conversation starter, and Clay needed one. He didn't want to be awkward today and drive Zeus away, especially after the way Scout had jumped away from him.

Zeus' hands rose and fell. "I didn't know it either until last night. But who doesn't love some unexpected heat?" Zeus' expression completely matched the sexual innuendo.

Still, he was damnably likable. "I'm sure there're a few people out there."

"True." Zeus' gaze flickered down Clay's body before returning to hold Clay's stare. "I haven't seen you in a bit. You drive-by dropped a funny movie quote on me and then never returned to my club."

Heat exploded through Clay's face. He hated his light coloration that showed every blush, but damn. The last time he had seen Zeus, Clay had made an idiot of himself by trying to join a conversation by reciting a line from a movie. Everyone had looked at him like the idiot he was, and Clay hadn't found the bravery to return to the kink club Zeus ran.

There was no avoiding being directly called out. "Yeah. Sorry about that. I'm awkward when... well, I'm just awkward."

Zeus smiled like he enjoyed the fuck out of himself. "You're adorable. That movie line never gets less funny, by the way. I'm sorry I didn't react differently. You caught me off guard, and—truth be told—I didn't want you to get friendly with the men talking to me. You're a giver. They're takers. All it would take was a few minutes with you, and you'd have three inferior men nipping at your heels."

Clay was oddly fascinated. Of course, Zeus was talking, and he was so pretty. It was hard to look away when the urge to pet him was so strong. "That reminds me. Why were they there? I thought Ridge and Shadow's reception was a private event."

Zeus nodded. "They work at the club. Shadow has been a member there for a while. The three wanted to celebrate the newlyweds."

"That makes sense. I'm still considering a membership, by the way. But I'm not sure if I'm a good fit since I'm not sure I fit in anywhere." Clay didn't even add a nervous laugh. Zeus was easy to talk to. Clay couldn't explain why. It was like Zeus screamed zero judgment. For Clay, that was a breath of fresh air at the moment. Between losing Fabrice's friendship and Scout only wanting to be friends, while simultaneously fucking with Clay's head, Clay wanted to sit with someone simple who meant nothing to him. Even in his head, that sounded like an asshole thing to admit, but it was true. Zeus and he would never be anything. He fully recognized that now.

"You fit with me. We should go to lunch."

"I just had breakfast." Clay's gaze shot in Scout's direction. He blinked. Scout and Tracker were gone. His chest hurt. Scout hadn't even said goodbye. It was almost like he didn't want anyone to think they were even real friends or anything. He was just teaching the Scout method of shooting. Otherwise, Clay meant nothing.

He met Zeus' stare. "I can get a drink while you eat."

Zeus tossed a muscular arm over Clay's shoulders and steered him toward the door. "You got a car here I can drive? If so, you can get plastered while I make sure you get home safely."

Clay laughed. If Scout didn't want him, Clay would not be the loser who refused to accept they were only fuck buddies. But he would be damned if he sat around pining. "This sounds like you intend to take advantage of me."

A sexy rumble of laughter fell from perfect lips and caressed Clay's ears. "Nah." He paused walking for a moment to meet Clay's stare. "When I take you, I want you sober. I want you present for every moment and thinking about me for the rest of your life."

Goddamn. Clay's mouth was dry.

Zeus went back to heading out. "Today, you drink and talk. I think you need that more than anything else I can give you. So, car?" He glanced Clay's way with raised eyebrows.

For the first time, Clay stared into those stunning light gray eyes, and he saw the real Zeus. "I've got what you need." Even Clay didn't know how he meant the statement. There was an SUV they could use, but Clay wasn't unaware of how he sounded. If Zeus kept being real with him, maybe Clay could shake Scout. He doubted it. Scout was all the way under his skin. But the one thing Clay knew above all others, from years of lived experience, he couldn't make anyone love him. Clay was sick of trying.

Chapter Eight

THE ROOM SPUN A little above him. Clay put one foot on the floor, hoping to make it stop. He closed his eyes for extra effort when that old trick didn't totally do the job. Everything about the day flashed through his mind in rapid succession, from breakfast to late-night dancing. Clay was glad he had let Zeus talk him into spending the day with him. Every hour had been a lot of fun. For the first time in a long time, Clay had let go of a lot of heavy things in his life.

It hadn't taken Zeus long to realize Clay saw through his ploys. From that moment, despite the occasional slip, Zeus had dropped the act. The man behind the sexual god was actually a pretty great guy. They hadn't talked about anything heavy, but somehow, they still managed to spend the entire day talking nonstop. Even when they had gone dancing, they spent so much time yelling over the music, they ended up in a quiet corner to keep their conversation alive. For the first time in a long time, Clay felt like he had made a real friend. No undertones beyond the habits that had been beaten into Zeus. Honestly, Clay hadn't wanted the night to end, but he couldn't stay out forever.

Despite the distractions Zeus provided, Clay hadn't completely pushed Scout from his mind. The way Scout had looked at him before they were interrupted wouldn't leave Clay. Too much thinking had him down a dozen rabbit holes. He had made some self-discoveries.

Before giving in to temptation with Scout, even before the first time Scout had kissed him, Clay had felt more for Scout than he had wanted to admit to himself. They had spent a lot of time together training. There had been countless nights where they got nothing done from spending the entire time joking, playing, and exchanging stories. Nothing too deep. Nothing about the past. Every story they told were things that happened after becoming adults. There had been times when Scout had corrected his stance. Times when he spoke close to Clay's ears. Clay hadn't wanted to admit how those nights affected him. It wasn't until he spent the day with Zeus, doing basically the same thing as he had with Scout, that Clay recognized how different the experience was. With Scout, Clay had always felt like they were working toward something bigger. Clay hadn't realized it because he had nothing to compare their relationship to. Fabrice had always been someone Clay loved. He understood now that love jumbled inside him sometimes. Clay desperately wanted what he saw between Beau and Kylo and the heat everyone felt between Henry and Field. He wanted something real. But Clay had never been taught how to find that for himself. He didn't always understand social cues. Other people made reading situations look easy. Nothing about any type of relationship came easy to him. Until two very different feelings toward people—like Scout and Zeus—had slapped him in the face, Clay hadn't fully understood why Scout's kiss had nearly sent him running. He should have kept going because Clay was ridiculously in love with Scout. Nothing could come from it but massive heartache, because if Clay knew nothing else, he knew Scout didn't feel the same.

Clay crossed his arms over his chest, protecting his heart. He was actually always pathetic. That knowledge hurt the most. Clay had prayed for Fabrice to love him. He had begged the universe for one night with Zeus. At the end of the day, here he was: one foot on the floor, room spinning, and physically trying to squash his dumbass heart. Sometimes, there wasn't enough therapy in the world.

Clay's phone chirped. With a groan, he rolled to his side and dug out his phone from his back pocket. The move reminded him he had fallen across the bed with no prep to go to sleep. Clay hoped Beau didn't need anything. It was two in the morning. He was fucked up. Nothing good could come of that combo.

Jett: *Did you make it to your room okay? I saw you come in with Zeus. You looked a little out of it.*

Great. He evidently looked like shit. Clay held the phone close to his face and tried to type. He wasn't sure he pulled it off.

Clay: *Yep. I'm in bed.*

The phone immediately dinged again. Clay huffed. Jett knew he was drunk. Damn.

Jett: *Don't tease me like that.*

Clay snorted and tossed his phone onto the bedside table. He was surrounded by relentless flirts. Clay gracelessly climbed from the bed. His legs twisted in the sheets. He didn't even remember messing up the covers. Clay barely stopped himself from landing on his face. The quick movement it took to keep him upright had Clay's head spinning faster.

"Whoa." Clay immediately fell across the bed again.

"Damn, beautiful. What have you done to yourself?"

The question barely penetrated Clay's hazy mind. He wanted to flirt and lure Scout into bed. Instead, he passed out.

Clay looked so adorable when Scout
tucked him into bed. Even in his sleep,
he looked drunk. The sight was so hi-
lariously cute that Scout couldn't look
away. Scout debated leaving, but he
would never forgive himself if Clay died
in the middle of the night from alcohol
poisoning.

Scout was already dressed for bed. He
had lain awake until Clay came tum-
bling in. The idea that Clay had spent
the entire day with Zeus was more than
a little under his skin. When Zeus arrived, it was like the guy couldn't see
anyone other than Clay. He hadn't even
acknowledged that Scout was in the
room. Walking away, leaving those two

alone, had murdered Scout inside. But Scout didn't want to act like a jealous idiot, and Tracker had asked for help to set up his gear. It seemed that turning his back for two minutes was all it had taken for Zeus to steal Clay. Of course, Scout wasn't the least bit surprised. Zeus was who he was. Unfortunately, it looked as if Zeus genuinely liked Clay. That meant Scout didn't stand a chance. Knowing that wouldn't stop Scout from pursuing Clay. Scout wasn't a quitter. Clay was his, even if he didn't realize it, and Scout wasn't backing down.

Scout turned the lights out and crawled beneath the covers with Clay. No sooner than his head hit the pillow, Clay's phone chirped loudly, startling the fuck out of him. He jumped up to silence the device. Scout got to it just in time to see the message on the face before the words faded away.

Jett: *Sorry if I went too far.*

For a moment, Scout's eye twitched so hard, he thought he'd lost vision in one eye. How did Jett go too far? Goddamn it. Clay was out of his sight for a single day, and everyone decided to shoot their shot. Scout turned the volume down until the tiny speaker symbol X'd out. With that done, Scout circled the bed again. He lifted the covers, and another chirp cut through the dark. Scout froze. Confusion kept him in place before he realized the notification was his. He rushed to his phone. It was rare for anyone to text him, much less in the middle of the night.

Tracker: *Are you up for a last-minute job?*

Scout furrowed his forehead as he read. It wasn't like them to be spontaneous. Spontaneous got people killed.

Scout: *First off, I thought we were on vacation. Second, what happened to training for each job for weeks?*

He watched the little dots jump while Tracker typed.

Tracker: *There's no way we could've prepped for this. Jay is back in town. He has Commander Kuznetsov with him.*

Scout's blood ran cold. He saw red. Commander Kuznetsov had been the man in charge of the program. He wasn't the head, but he was the iron grip. Kuznetsov was also the monster who visited Rain almost nightly, forcing him to do the worst of things. The time had come. He was within their reach.

Scout: *Give me five to get dressed and I'll meet you.*

Tracker: *Sounds good. Let's end this.*

Scout forgot everything but his mission. The time had come for retribution.

Tracker chewed the side of his finger-nail, waiting for the guys to gear up. He hated pulling everyone out of bed. More than that, he loathed jobs that had a high chance of going sideways. This rush wasn't their M.O., but this job was different. It was personal. If there was a single chance they could get to

Kuznetsov, they had to take it. They deserved to watch the life leave his eyes.

"You've got this."

The sound of Zeus' voice startled Tracker. He had forgotten Zeus was there.
Zeus had likely never had that happen
to him before. He was probably used to
being the greatest god in every room.
Zeus had been created to be perfection,
and he was. That was why Tracker
was one of the rare people who wasn't
attracted to Zeus like that. They were
friends. They had a hell of a lot in com-
mon. In fact, Zeus had found them after
their escape from the program because
he was such a huge computer nerd. He
had set up a computer program, one he
had created himself, to let him know
if anyone searched online for anyone
in or from the program. A couple of

years after they ran away, Tracker had hacked some systems, looking for people like them. Zeus had shown up on their doorstep ready to kill them to keep his freedom. Of course, what he found was a bunch of guys just like him. Now, they had come together to create a DNA database. They had all been genetically engineered before the fertilized eggs had been dumped into a group of women. Whoever stuck was the next generation of super spies. When Zeus and Ridge decided they wanted to know if they were twins, since they were practically photocopies of each other, they had uncovered a whole warren of rabbit holes to go through.

Tracker flashed Zeus a tight smile. "Why do you look so unbothered? I imagine you have a bone or two to pick with that sadistic bastard too."

Zeus' current calm demeanor with zero artifice was a rare sight. "Your plan is solid. He won't get away."

While sitting in a dark van in the garage, with nothing but a lit computer screen highlighting them, it hit Tracker how close they had become over the years. During the past week of studying the odds of how many of them were related—while waiting on DNA results—their friendship had truly grown. They had geeked out together several times over the years, getting together to share their work. But this project was different. This was about their past and their future. The waiting was an exercise in patience neither of them had on this matter. He had been with his brothers for decades, and—somehow—Tracker felt closer to Zeus than any of them. Zeus was his best friend.

Tracker leaned back in his seat, settling in to draw some comfort from Zeus' presence. Before he said a word, the side door slid open, and the guys poured in. It wasn't their specialized vehicle from back home. The van was just wheels in Beau's garage that Tracker had hurriedly made his own while waiting. With Zeus' help, of course. Still, they could make it work.

Edge stuck his head between the front seats. "Tidy, Crisp, and Scout are already headed that way. They'll drop Scout a street over so he can walk the block. If anyone can tell if this is a trap, it's him. Tidy and Crisp will park nearby and wait for the cleanup call."

Tracker nodded. Everything inside him wound tight. He wondered if he would hyperventilate before they even made it to the small rental house where their target slept. Tracker was damn glad Zeus was at his side. For some reason, Tracker believed to his soul that Zeus would never allow anything bad to happen to him. He supposed time would tell.

Chapter Nine

IT WAS A GREAT night for a walk. Scout dressed like a jogger. He had earbuds in, keeping track of the gang, while he jogged a little before slowing back down to a walk after cars passed. Scout kept his eyes peeled and ears open to Tracker. The adrenaline had died down a bit. He was a professional. This was where Scout shone.

Since he hadn't gotten a chance to scope the neighborhood ahead of time, he didn't know if there were any out-of-place vehicles. It was an upper-class subdivision. Scout eyed each car, making sure it matched the class level. This was definitely one of those places where people weren't rich enough not to care what their neighbors thought. It was a keeping-up-with-the-Joneses situation. The only out-of-price-range vehicle he found was likely their target's rental. It was so strange to picture such an evil figure driving a ten-year-old family sedan. Even though they were here to destroy the man who had raised them in so much cruelty, Scout still fought wayward thoughts. What if his brothers and he could finally strike out on their own? How many of his brothers would choose to keep the family together? What if they were an actual blood family? Tracker worked to find out, and it had Scout a little on edge. So many things could go wrong thanks to those results. What if Ridge and Shadow turned out to be brothers? They were married and deeply in love. That knowledge would rip them apart. What if damn near everyone was related in some way while he was the only outlier? Would everyone eventually push him out and make him feel less than? Sometimes he already felt that way. A set of shadows moved along the dark edge of the rental home where Kuznetsov stayed. There was no glow of LED lights, peeking through the dark. Horror struck. It wasn't their team.

Scout pushed the button on his earbud. "Guys. We have a problem."

"You have your own troubles to worry about." The thick Russian accent accompanied a knife to his throat, and another poised at his kidney.

Scout didn't respond. He had always known he would likely die at the hands of the program. Scout wouldn't give them the satisfaction of seeing him care. But fuck, for real, he would miss the life he could have built with Clay. He marched in the direction he was told. Scout followed every command. Once inside, he felt sick as fuck at the sight that met him. If Jay was still alive at Kuznetsov's feet, he wouldn't be for long, judging by the amount of blood that coated the floor. No doubt he had been tortured until he led Kuznetsov to them. If that was the case, Jay had really taken a lot before breaking. He hated knowing Jay was likely just like them, dying to be free. Scout supposed he was now.

Cold, sick blue eyes looked his way as he was steered into the room. His brothers were all there, even Tidy and Crisp.

Scout had no idea how this had happened beneath his nose. He had been on his toes, knowing the importance of this job. Then again, Kuznetsov had trained them. There was likely no move they could make he wouldn't anticipate.

With his hands clasped behind his back, his chest out, and hair perfectly brushed, Kuznetsov didn't look his age. The guy bordered on elderly. Yet he looked no more than forty-five. There wasn't a single frail thing about him. Apparently, evil kept people young.

"Look how grown all of you are." Kuznetsov's greedy gaze moved to Rain. He could hardly show his true interest in front of his men, and they were everywhere. Unfortunately, knowing the truth, Scout wanted to vomit at the twisted light in the commander's eyes each time he focused on Rain. A full team held guns on the room while Scout's brothers stood proud, holding their LED masks. Not a single one showed an ounce of fear.

Rain refused to look at Kuznetsov. It was a bold move, considering they all knew Rain was truly Kuznetsov's target. He had lost his favorite toy. Kuznetsov would not let such a beautiful prize slip away. Tonight had always been inevitable. As long as Kuznetsov lived, he would hunt Rain. At the thought of beauty, Scout's gaze skimmed the room again. Zeus wasn't there. That thought was gone in an instant when Kuznetsov opened his mouth.

He stood toe to toe with Rain. "Choose. These men ran away because of you, so you choose which one dies first."

Rain finally met Kuznetsov's stare. "Me." His expression said he had made peace with dying.

An evil-sounding laugh rolled through the room, sending chills down Scout's spine. "No. This won't be that simple. You will live a very long life back home where you belong, knowing all these men died because of you. Choose."

"Me."

Rage passed over Kuznetsov's features at Rain's continued defiance. Kuznetsov's obvious impatience to have Rain alone in his clutches took control. He looked toward the man holding the knife against Scout's neck.

He didn't know why he had been chosen to go first, but Scout braced himself to die. Scout far preferred that end over being forced back to Russia. He wished he had kissed Clay goodbye, though. Not telling Clay how he felt was his only true regret. The familiar sound of a bullet cutting through the air buzzed past Scout's ear. The knife fell away. Before Scout had time to turn, his abductor hit the ground dead. A round bullet hole in the dead center of his forehead was barely a passing observation before men dropped one by one in such rapid succession, no one even had time to shout. By the time Clay stepped fully into the room, Scout's brain finally caught up with reality. Only Kuznetsov was left standing beyond Scout's team.

Clay didn't take his eyes off Kuznetsov. It took Scout a full three seconds to realize Kuznetsov clutched a bloody hand with missing fingers against his chest. A gun had been shot from his hold.

Scout couldn't tear his gaze away from Clay. He had done it. Clay had used Scout's method, and he was still drunk as fuck. That didn't stop him from looking sexy as hell. Goddamn, Scout had never wanted anyone more.

Beau strolled into the room with Henry watching his back. As one of the world's most dangerous crime lords, Beau looked the part. Salt and pepper hair, cut in a way that screamed money, joined a flawless and expensive suit. Deadly-looking eyes skimmed the room. He released a tired-sounding sigh that sounded loud as hell in the otherwise silent living room.

Being the bastard he was, Kuznetsov didn't give them the gift of hearing him scream. His jaw flexed, though. He wanted to show his pain.

Beau took a turn around the room under the guise of looking over the dead bodies scattered in nearly a perfect circle. Scout was the eagle eyes, though. He saw the way Beau reassured himself none of them were hurt.

Beau spoke as he walked. "I thought we had an unspoken truce of sorts, Kuznetsov. Your country continues to receive my services, as long as my boys are left in peace." He stopped three feet from the commander. If Kuznetsov wasn't shaking inside, Scout was on his behalf. Beau was truly a terrifying man. "A small part of me wants to send you home to face the wrath of losing my supply." A smile so evil that Scout literally stepped back stretched Beau's lips. There could be no doubt they stared at the man who had taken the weapons trade by force before he even turned eighteen. Here was the man everyone feared. "But I won't risk you somehow weaseling out of your punishment. You look like someone who weasels."

Kuznetsov spat at Beau's feet. "Fuck you."

The spit missed, but Henry didn't. He punched Kuznetsov in the kidney hard enough to take the commander to his knees. That one got a small cry. Scout wanted so many more. He needed to hear every pleading word and pained scream. They were owed that much.

"No, commander. Fuck you." Beau sounded colder than ice. He glanced toward the doorway, where more guards waited for orders. "Pick him up. You know where to take him. My boys deserve some retribution." He turned a malicious look Kuznetsov's way. "My boys are owed their pound of flesh, and they'll have it."

Heavy emotions poured through Scout. The time had come for vengeance, and he didn't know how to feel.

The moment Kuznetsov was on his way, chained, and out the door, Clay headed his way. "Holy shit, Scout. You okay? He didn't get a chance to do anything to you, right?" He inspected Scout's neck like a worried mother.

Scout set his hand on Clay's chest, trying to physically calm him. "I'm okay. You were right on time. Thank you for that. You were badass, which I'm learning is your natural state."

A bright smile lit Clay's face. "What are friends for?"

Scout shook his head. "We were never just friends." He closed the gap between them and claimed the kiss he had feared he would never have again. It didn't last as long as he wanted, but they weren't alone. That thought had him glancing over Clay's shoulder. His brothers stood stoic, waiting for Scout to join them in closing a chapter of their lives. He met Clay's gaze. "I have to go with them."

"I know." There was no judgment in his eyes. Clay understood.

"When it's over, I'll come to you."

A sweet smile touched Clay's lips. "There's no rush. I'm not going any-where."

A weight lifted from Scout's chest. Clouds parted in his mind, showing him everything he had missed. Clay had been waiting for Scout to see it was them. They were a they. Clay hadn't been entertaining the idea of choosing anyone else. They were real, and Scout had been too blind to see it.

Clay had expected the wait for Scout to come to him would be absolute hell, but—oddly—it wasn't. Not only was he half-dead after being pulled from his drunken sleep, but the adrenaline caught him. Clay went home, showered, brushed his teeth, and then died. He had gone dead to the world for fifteen hours with no interruptions. While he had been a little bummed Scout wasn't in bed with him when his eyes opened, he was okay. Clay understood the emotional turmoil Scout and his family were enduring under the circumstances. Any discussion Scout and Clay needed to have would still be there when Scout finished closing the book on his past.

Clay ate alone in the dining room. After sleeping the day away, he had missed all major meals. Thankfully, there were leftovers in the fridge. All the kitchen staff had finished for the night. All Clay had was food and silence.

"You're avoiding me."

Fabrice's voice nearly made Clay jump out of his skin. Clay had been too lost in thought to notice his appearance.

He cleared his throat. "Why would you think that?"

A sad smile touched Fabrice's lips as he pulled out a chair at the table and sat. "Because I deserve it and you never miss breakfast two days in a row, much less lunch and dinner."

Clay wouldn't deny him deserving it, but the rest wasn't what Fabrice thought. "I spent the day with Zeus yesterday. Today, I slept the whole day."

Fabrice's light blue stare moved over Clay's face, as if weighing Clay's honesty. "I guess being the talk of the household probably is exhausting."

Clay's eyebrows rose. "What's that supposed to mean?" He hadn't meant the question to sound so accusatory. They just weren't in a good place, and Fabrice's mixed accent made it hard for Clay to decipher his tone.

A tiny smile popped to Fabrice's lips. "Apparently, you really have been training these last few months. Word is you're a real badass now."

Great. Everyone was talking about him. "I've always been a badass."

Fabrice's grin grew. He chuckled. "I thought that one would get a rise out of you. Seriously, though. It sounds as though you saved the day last night. Beau hasn't stopped bragging and saying he knew he had been right to hinge his plans on you. Apparently, even plastered, you're easily one of the best out there."

Clay shook his head. That was twice Clay couldn't picture Beau singing his praises. At this point, Fabrice had to be making things up. "I'm not special. Scout is just a good teacher."

The happiness left Fabrice's expression. "Speaking of Scout, I should've stayed out of that. You're my best friend. For me, there's nothing worth losing that. Can we pretend I didn't say anything? The last two days have been hell, knowing you don't want to be my friend anymore."

Everything inside Clay softened. "You're my best friend. I'll always want you in my life. Tormenting you while you work is one of my favorite parts of the day."

They shared a smile. At the same moment, they leaned toward each other and reached for the other. Their hug felt like a healing embrace. Spending the day with Zeus, soul-searching, had Clay making several self-discoveries. It helped that Zeus was a master deprogrammer. Apparently, breaking through inner barriers was more like breaking spies' triggers than one would think. Truthfully, it was no wonder Zeus was such a sought-after dom at that kink club of his. He saw people. Clay had spent his life scared of losing the only love he had: Fabrice. But Clay had never loved him in a way that kept a couple together forever. Until now, Clay had nothing to compare types of love. He felt the difference now.

Fabrice sat back and swiped his eyes. "Are you eating that cold?"

Clay shrugged. "I had to drag myself out of bed. I didn't have the energy to heat it. But I'm almost done now. It's fine."

Fabrice shook his head. "At least let me get you some dessert."

Clay's stomach growled in epic timing at the mention of something sweet. "There's dessert?" Cooking was Fabrice's love language. Clay didn't mind reaching for this particular olive branch.

Fabrice stood. "There's always dessert."

Scout strolled into the dining room. He looked fresh from the shower.

Fabrice held out his chair for Scout. "I'll bring two plates."

Clay flashed Fabrice a grateful smile. He understood what that cost. But there was no time like the present to accept they would never be more than friends.

Scout nodded his appreciation. "Thanks. You going to join us?"

Fabrice looked between them. Clay practically felt him searching for an excuse.

Beau chose that moment to appear with Henry right behind him. He focused on Clay as he pulled out a chair and sat. "Good. You're up." His gaze flickered Fabrice's way. "Grab that cake and some plates. You'll be joining us too."

Fabrice dipped his chin. "Oui, Monsieur." He backed from the room with the grace of a professional.

Beau's light brown eyes focused on Clay again. "I didn't get a chance to talk to you last night." Beau chuckled. "Not that I'm sure you would've remembered anything said."

Clay smiled. It was a genuine gesture. He cared about Beau. "You're probably right."

Fabrice reappeared with the cake. While he cut, Scout stood and passed around silverware and empty plates until everyone was settled.

Beau waited until they had enjoyed a few bites of Fabrice's flawless ganache-covered cake before speaking again. "As you know, I've delegated a majority of my work to others over the last year, attempting to be semi-retired."

Clay nodded. "You've been surprisingly still. I didn't think you would ever get this much free time."

An expression overcame Beau's features that showed more and more: a man in love. "Kylo is worth it."

"He's perfect for you." Clay hadn't found a chance to say that until now.

A fatherly smile Clay had only ever seen Beau use for his sons stretched his lips. There was never a moment when Beau wasn't terrifying. Sometimes, he looked a little closer to human. This was one of those times. "I got lucky when he found me. But we're here about you now."

Oh, that couldn't be good.

Beau must have seen something in his expression. He held up his hand briefly. "I don't know what you're thinking, but it's likely wrong. Even I didn't see this decision coming before this trip."

Clay breathed easier.

Beau kept talking. "I've always been proud as hell of you. You grew up at my feet every bit as my sons." Beau glanced Fabrice's way. "Both of you."

A huge grin split Fabrice's face. Considering Fabrice's grandfather was one of those screaming, angry chefs, Clay didn't imagine anyone had ever told Fabrice they were proud of him.

"I said that to say this: you can say no to this plan. This isn't me giving you an order. It's an offer."

Clay really hoped he wasn't about to get asked to kill anyone else this week. He was kind of tired.

Unaware of the storm he caused inside Clay, Beau pushed on. "Kylo is happy here, but my living here full time isn't an option at this time. However, I'm always at his mercy, so we'll be here more often. Likely, we'll rotate months or go with six months at a time. Either way, things will run smoother if we have a skeleton crew here on a permanent basis." Beau's gaze grew more intense. "You've proven yourself to be the best of our chosen family. Under Henry, of course."

Henry laughed as if there was never any doubt on that matter.

"I'd like you to stay here and run the crew. You'll be equal to Henry in terms of position and pay."

Clay sat frozen. He wasn't sure he even blinked. This was Beau handing Clay his biggest dream. Except he had finally won Scout, and Scout would want to stay with his family.

Oblivious to his inner turmoil, Beau continued to lay out his future. "Pierre has decided he is bored with retirement and would like to return part time."

Fabrice immediately looked devastated. He had held the head chef position for only a little over a year. Now he would be forced to step aside.

Beau didn't give him time to simmer. "You'll stay here, Fabrice. That is, if you'd like to keep your current position. If not, I can send Pierre, and you can keep the kitchen back home. But with a crew here, they'll need a full-time head chef, and you're the only one I trust."

Fabrice looked shell-shocked.

Without permission from his brain, Clay's gaze slid Scout's way. Not only would Scout not be here, but Clay would be here with someone who Scout had already shown some jealousy toward.

Scout took his hand under the table and squeezed. He didn't look at Clay.

Beau's gaze bounced between them. "Obviously, your man can stay as well. I'm not one to split a set."

Clay smiled, but he didn't feel it. He shouldn't be surprised that his dream job might be a nightmare. Life didn't believe in pity.

"You'll have time to think about it. We still have several weeks before we head back to California."

Henry jumped in. "I'd appreciate it if you let me know at least a couple of weeks ahead of time. If we need to choose someone else, we need time to discuss our options."

Clay nodded along, as if he wasn't completely floored by the massive decision he needed to make. He could have his dream, or he could have Scout. Clay seriously doubted he would have both.

By the time they finally got a minute alone, Scout was ready to scream. He needed time with Clay. The last—at least—forty-eight hours had been such a rollercoaster of emotions, Scout wanted to drop. He couldn't do that until they talked.

When the last wisp of anyone else's presence went out the door, Clay snagged the collar of Scout's shirt and pulled him in for a kiss. Clay touched Scout's face lovingly. Suddenly, Scout was as close to crying as he had been in a long time. Scout still couldn't believe he hadn't felt the reverence each time Clay touched him. Even when Clay was rough, he acted like the world was about to end and Clay had to get one more chance to be connected with Scout.

Clay pulled away and kissed Scout's forehead. He sat back, setting Scout free. "Tell me everything. Are you okay? Is it over?"

Before Scout could respond, Crisp strolled into the room. He barely glanced between them. "Don't mind me, guys. I heard there was cake."

Scout made it half a second into watching Crisp shovel cake onto two plates.

He stood and held his hand out to Clay. Clay didn't hesitate to take it. Together, they made their way through the house and into Scout's bedroom. They climbed onto the bed and sat cross-legged, facing each other. It was as if they shared the same brain for a minute—like they made silent plans.

Scout didn't know where to start, so he just opened his mouth and words spilled out. "You know I'm all about communication. But sometimes I forget you can't read my thoughts. Well, most of the time, really. In hindsight—" Scout ran his hands up Clay's thighs. He kept his gaze on Clay's lap. Scout felt at sea. The perfect words wouldn't come to him. "We decided—as a group—to leave the commander with Rain. He's owed every drop of blood that vile piece of shit has."

"I saw the way he looked at Rain. Even three sheets to the wind, the way his eyes devoured Rain sent chills down my spine. The way Rain held himself—like a man holding his pride as armor—was heartbreaking. I'm guessing Rain is the real reason you guys have stuck together?"

A sad smile tugged at Scout's lips. "Some of it, yeah. Also, none of us know how to be normal." Scout lifted his chin and met Clay's stare. "We don't know how to do anything else but kill. Not really. Rain and Shadow have ballet, and Tracker could be anything. He's a genius. But for the most part, we're all just broken. Together, we don't see all the cracks. It wasn't until I silently fell in love with you that I realized how dysfunctional I really am."

Clay's lips parted in surprise, but he didn't interrupt.

Scout appreciated the hell out of that. If he stopped now, he didn't know what would happen. Maybe he would lose his nerve. "That day you caught me looking into your past, you were so fucking amazing at talking about things. You were beautifully open with me. I guess I thought if you wanted me beyond the bedroom, you'd say it. You didn't, and I kept reinforcing how we were friends." He knew he had to look as defeated as he felt. Even he didn't know where he was going with this. "I don't know."

"You're right." Clay's response surprised the frustration from Scout. "I should've said what I wanted that first night, but I was scared to lose what little I had of us. Until last night, I thought I was afraid because I was gun-shy. For a while, a couple of years back, I thought maybe the love I felt for Fabrice was romantic." A wry smile crossed his features. "It never was. I won't go into all the many reasons I probably need therapy. But that was just one of the few times I thought I meant more to someone than I did. You kept calling me your friend, and it had my head all fucked. I kind of went into self-destruct mode. But then I saw that knife against your throat, and I knew I had to tell you how I feel while I still have a chance with you." He took a deep breath. The way he held Scout's stare had Scout holding his breath. "We spent all those months training, and I don't know. Obviously, from the first time I saw you, I thought you were gorgeous. Then I got to know you, and I was hooked. But you weren't showing any signs you felt the same, and then—"

"That's on my programming." He hated to interrupt Clay, but he couldn't let Clay think he was cold. "I can't seem to change some things programmed into me. Everything I feel stays locked behind my teeth, and no matter how hard I try, I can't force words to go past my lips. I know I'm not explaining myself well. But when I saw the way you looked at Zeus at that wedding reception, I knew I had to do something. So I acted, and you stopped talking to me, and everything inside me withdrew, but I couldn't stop trying to be near you. I know I'm rambling."

Clay moved to his knees and toppled Scout. Scout froze, transfixed by the emotions that stared down at him as

Clay crawled on top of him. "I love you. That's what I should've said that very first night in bed. I'm in love with you. With you, I didn't even need you to kiss me or for us to make love. I fell in love with the guy who showed up every night; even when I went to that kink club, you waited at home for me. When I came here, there you were again. Right by my side. We were always meant to be." He lowered his weight on Scout. "Now I just want to hold you and try to let go of the fear of you almost dying. While I do, you can tell me as much of your feelings as you want about this commander thing."

Scout wrapped his arms around Clay as Clay settled in for cuddles. A smile snapped to his lips. "I literally never dreamed I'd have this. We were trained from day one not to need anyone, want anyone, or feel anything at all, really. I was supposed to grow up and hit the streets running as a cold, emotionless machine. Only duty to my country existed." Scout heard his Russian accent deepen. He was tired. Scout was always less guarded on the edge of sleep. "Now, all I can think about is how much I love this. I'm thinking about snuggling, for fuck's sake. You're real, and you can't know." Scout didn't know to finish that sentence. Clay simply couldn't know. He was supposed to be this heartless thing, and Clay didn't let that happen.

Clay shifted onto his hip, keeping his leg thrown over Scout. He grabbed a handful of covers and pulled the blankets over them. "You need sleep." His lips swiped Scout's mouth. "I'll hold you and keep you safe."

Scout couldn't stop smiling even as his eyelids grew heavier and heavier. They would be okay. Clay loved him. Everything else would fall into place.

Chapter Ten

SOFT KISSES ON HIS neck pulled Clay from his sleep. Without opening his eyes, he ran his hand through Scout's hair. He couldn't believe he had slept again after the fifteen-hour marathon, but he had a feeling he had been mentally drained for much longer than he realized. Clay loved the way Scout smelled—like some sort of exotic fruit straight from the shower. His hair was wet, and Clay didn't care. He could run his fingers through the wet locks all day. Scout's mouth moved to Clay's chest. A needy moan escaped Clay. He still hadn't opened his eyes, and he was rock hard. Scout did something to him no one else ever had—on the inside where no one could see. He touched a part of Clay that hadn't been released before him. Clay had a feeling if anything happened to them, he would never feel this much passion again.

Clay heard the crinkle of a condom packet. He peeked open one eye.

Scout held his stare as he brought the wrapper to his mouth and used his teeth to open it. His gaze moved to Clay's cock as he rolled the condom down Clay's length.

"I'm about to use you."

Clay closed his eyes. "I'm here for it."

A wicked chuckle filled the air.

Clay got goosebumps at the sound. It seemed Scout had no qualms with

Clay's laziness. Fuck, Scout just did it for him. He brought Clay's senses to life. Clay conserved his energy. Plus, he kind of wanted to see exactly how Scout liked it. Clay needed to know every detail of Scout because—one way or another—he intended to keep him.

Scout sat on Clay's dick.

Clay was awake. "Mhmm. Fuck. You feel good."

"You stole my line." Scout lifted and lowered himself.

A pant burst from Clay. He wasn't in control. That went against Clay's nature, but he let Scout take charge... until he couldn't any longer. Clay flipped, audibly knocking the air from Scout's lungs as he hit the bed. With Scout staring up at him—wide-eyed and ready—Clay held him in the position he liked and took Scout's ass. Scout looked half insane with lust.

Clay felt all the control flow back his way. He studied Scout's face and fucked him the way Scout seemed to be the most into it. Clay really couldn't see himself with anyone else. Not only did he love just sitting and talking to Scout, but he had also never had sex this good.

"You look so beautiful beneath me. I'm so fucking in love with you."

Scout released a loud moan. He writhed like a sexy mess.

Clay lost his train of thought as Scout's greedy asshole overtook his mind. He turned his chin up and closed his eyes, savoring every second.

"Fuck, baby. You're so goddamn sexy inside me. I can't take it."

At Scout's desperate tone, Clay dropped his gaze to meet his stare. A flush covered Scout's cheeks. He fought visibly for breath. So much lust stared up at Clay that Clay had to grind his back teeth to keep from blowing right then.

Scout tensed and Clay gasped. He was stealing Clay's soul. Then Scout's entire body jerked, and his spine left the bed in an arch that Clay knew would live in his head as the sexiest sight. Scout whined and cum coated his stomach. Clay lost it. He held Scout in place and pounded him through an orgasm so hard, Clay forgot how to breathe. By the time he made it to the final twitches, his lungs burned. Clay sucked in a deep breath. He sounded as if he had run for miles.

"Holy shit. Fuck, Scout. You make my dumb ass forget to breathe."

The way Scout's body shook with silent laughter was captivating to watch. Clay dropped and rolled to the side, landing next to Scout while still struggling to catch his breath.

Scout brushed his palm down Clay's side. "I swear you turn into someone else when you're inside me. You're almost scary with the way you watch me. Even though I'm not in danger of anything, except pulling something with how hard you make me come, you look at me like you can't decide between fucking me or killing me."

The statement swelled Clay's throat. "I don't mean to be so intense. You'll always be safe with me."

Scout turned serious. "Am I? It's hitting me how much you could wreck me. I've never felt this much for anyone or anything. If you take it away..." He shook his head. "I might do anything."

He sounded vulnerable and adrift, as if the thoughts running through his head terrified him. Clay stroked his face while holding his stare. "Same. No one would be safe."

One corner of Scout's mouth lifted in a hint of a smile. "That's probably not normal, but neither are we, so..." He shrugged.

Clay chuckled. He honestly loved this man. Maybe they were fucked up, but they would be a huge mess together. He hoped. Clay had a decision to make with this promotion. He didn't know what to do.

Even though he had just taken a shower, Scout needed another after the way Clay—once again—rocked him to his soul. Instead, they ended up sitting in the huge tub in Scout's bathroom. Facing each other, they relaxed, letting the hot water soothe their muscles. Scout felt like he had been holding himself stiff since he had met Clay. Now that the strain slowly released, he realized how much he had carried unnecessarily.

Clay's toe tickled Scout's elbow beneath the water.

Scout couldn't stop smiling. "You're lucky I'm not one of those people who hate feet."

Clay laughed. He sounded as happy as Scout felt. "If you were, I'd still touch you with them just to annoy you."

Damn, his face hurt from all the fucking smiling. "Fuck, dude. We're about to have the best life together."

Clay's smile slipped away.

Scout watched the discomfort take over every inch of Clay. A bad feeling squeezed his gut. "What?" He sounded more demanding than he meant, but fuck. Scout thought they had decided they were together.

A sad smile touched Clay's lips and disappeared just as quickly. "You heard Beau. He wants me to stay here, and—seriously—I'll go or stay wherever you are. But I have to admit, I want to stay. Living here has been my secret dream since the first time Beau brought me here. It's beautiful and peaceful. At least it was until I was forced to kill a bunch of people, but I really think that was a one-off. Not to mention, as dumb as it might sound, this kind of feels like my dad giving me a gift." Clay's smile slipped as he blushed at the admission; even the hot water couldn't hide it.

Scout had always had a hard time understanding why Ridge had never given up on Shadow. Even though Scout respected the hell out of Edge, he hadn't understood why Edge humbled the fuck out of himself with Mickey. He hadn't thought he would ever feel that much for anyone. In fact, he hadn't understood what they felt at all. Looking at Clay now, practically begging Scout to choose him, everything was clear. There was nothing he wouldn't do for Clay. That included leaving his family.

Scout tried to smile, but the moment felt too pivotal. "I only let you give me that entire rundown because I think you needed it off your chest. Obviously, I still haven't figured out how to express myself well when it comes to emotional things. Still, I thought you understood we stick together now. I go where you go and stay where you stay. You deserve this promotion and beautiful life here."

Clay bit his bottom lip. His expression screamed guilt. "Now I feel like I'm coming between your brothers and you. Like I'm making the decision to tear you apart."

He swore Clay wouldn't stop looking for cracks. It was slowly sinking in that Clay was even more insecure about this relationship than he let on.

Scout held out his hand. Clay accepted and moved to his side of the tub. He had to sit half on Scout's lap for them to fit, but that was the point. Scout needed to hold Clay. He kissed Clay's collarbone. "Please stop trying to convince yourself I don't want you forever. I may be emotionally ignorant, but I know my heart. Plus, you heard Beau. They'll be here half or more of the year. The guys can come if they want, and you know they will. We'll still see each other. They'd never expect me to choose them in this situation. Edge and Field have already pretty much announced they'd choose their husbands if put in that position. That's the way it's supposed to be."

Clay stared at him like his entire life hinged on Scout's every word. "You really want this, don't you?"

Scout couldn't stop his eye roll if he tried. "I'm about two seconds away from drowning you."

A smile snapped to Clay's lips. "Damn. It didn't take long for you to be ready to commit murder." He shifted and straddled Scout's lap. His expression turned vulnerable, but he never looked away from Scout. "I love you."

Scout didn't hesitate to return the words. "I love you too." He smiled. "Honestly, you'll probably get sick of me saying that."

Clay lowered his head. "Never."

When their lips met, the world shifted and clicked into place. Scout would never be alone again. Soon they would be practically alone in paradise—just them and this beautiful thing they built. He had never wanted to cry, laugh, and shout like he did at that moment. Scout had a genuine future headed his way. Thank fuck.

Chapter Eleven

AFTER SEVEN WEEKS OF loud dinners, laughter, and pool parties, as much as Clay enjoyed himself, he was ready for some quiet. It had been really nice, though. The Agafonov brothers had always made him feel like one of them. What Clay hadn't been prepared for was an overly relaxed Beau treating him like a son. Truth be told, he had a secret he would take to the grave. There was a lie he had kept up his entire life and always would. He had always seen Beau as a father. That admission—even to himself—was a bit humiliating. He was part of an army of people who would die for Beau. Well, the leader of an army now. Not that his exact position mattered. He wasn't supposed to need a family. Clay was supposed to be one of those men who kept their emotions bottled. But Beau had always treated him a lot like his sons, and that mattered to Clay. Clay didn't have Beau's sons' money and freedom. But in a drunken, drug-induced state once, back when Tabitha had still been alive and Beau had gone through a phase of joining her on the high side, Beau had told Clay something he likely didn't even recall. Beau told Clay he loved him like one of his own. He was sorry Clay hadn't been given the same life as Boone and Banks, but in the heart, he thought he had ruined them by spoiling them. They were addicts, like their mom, and didn't appreciate what they had. Of course, that was several years ago, long before Banks and Boone got their lives together. The three were still trying to work their way back to each other, but they hadn't given up. Clay knew they would be fine. Sometimes healing took a long time. In their case, they each had a lot to be sorry about and a ton of forgiveness to dish out. Clay had always been grateful to be left out of that mess, but yeah. Clay had carried that confession in his chest ever since. He didn't have a family. Clay wanted as much as he could get.

Tonight, he felt like a bit of an intruder. The Agafonov brothers sat in a big circle with their spouses along for the ride. It was their last night together before they left a brother behind.

Tracker stood. He held a bundle of envelopes. "It was probably shitty of me to hang on to these DNA results until the last minute. Honestly, I'm a little scared to share them. We've always been family without knowing our blood ties. I don't want that to change."

"Family isn't blood," Field said, cutting in.

Henry squeezed the shoulders of his massive, red-haired goofball husband. "Field is right. No amount of DNA can replace the life you all have shared. Blood won't change what no one can break."

A round of "damn straight" and other agreements grumbled through the room.

Tracker took a deep breath and let it out slowly. "Well, here we go." He moved from person to person, passing out sealed envelopes of results. He handed one to Clay. Clay's name was written on the outside and everything.

His fingers automatically closed around the envelope, but his confusion couldn't be hidden. "What's this?"

Tracker winked. "I didn't want you to feel left out."

To his shame, Clay went a little dim-witted at that wink. Tracker looked exactly like a really hot news anchor. He was always dressed on point and his hair was perfectly styled. Yet he looked completely comfortable in his high-dollar casual office attire.

A nervous-sounding laugh escaped Clay. "I'm a little scared to ask how you got my DNA."

Tracker's smile was filled with humor. He winked again and went back to his seat, where Zeus openly waited for his return.

"On three," Rain said when no one opened their results.

They exchanged glances, and everyone started slowly counting. When they reached three, they gently opened their results as if equally scared of what was inside. Clay didn't open his. He stared over Scout's shoulder. It was a detailed list. He had expected a random set of numbers they would have to decipher. Clay should have known Tracker would be more thorough. He had broken down everyone's results into an easy-to-read and understand document. Before he had time to read the first line, Zeus and Ridge shot to their feet and met halfway. To his surprise, they both had tears in their eyes as they hugged, babbling about how they had known it. They were twins. Actually, two of triplets. They had Edge on his feet as well when they quickly realized he was the third.

Clay couldn't help but smile. He went back to staring at Scout's list. Scout kind of stared into space, as if he locked up halfway through. Clay scanned the page for Scout's name. He matched with several names, and Clay quickly lost the plot when things turned into a rabbit hole. It looked like Shadow, Shore, and Scout were all brothers. He wondered if the S names were a coincidence or some deliberate way to keep track. Tracker, Field, and Foster were brothers and first cousins to Shadow, Shore, and Scout. Clay's eyes widened when he noticed Shadow and Rain were twins too, making Scout brothers with Rain as well. The lone ones out were Tidy and Crisp, who showed no relation to anyone else on the list.

Clay glanced around the room, trying to gauge everyone's reactions. Rain and Shadow both had their hands over their mouths while they stared at each other with tears running down their faces. After a moment, they looked Scout's way and then to Shore. None of them moved. It was as if shock had rendered them useless.

Field swiped his eyes but didn't look at anyone. Foster, who typically kept himself away from the group, looked totally unaffected.

Tidy and Crisp held hands and cried, but Crisp spoke up first. "It doesn't matter. You're still our brothers."

It hit Clay. They were always on the fringes, and this further divided them from the only family they had ever known.

Field finally stood. He headed their way and went down on his knees between their chairs. Belying their earlier statement, they ugly-cried the moment Field pulled them into a hug.

Clay glanced Austen, Henry, and Mickey's way. They looked how Clay felt—like they too had witnessed something they shouldn't have. But then another realization nearly took him out. They didn't have envelopes. Tracker had said he didn't want Clay to feel left out. Why didn't they have envelopes?

His gaze dropped to his lap, where the results he had been handed stared up at him.

Scout bumped shoulders with him. "Open it. What's the worst that could happen?"

A nervous chuckle burst from Clay. "I could open this and find out we're related."

Scout didn't roll his eyes, but Clay felt how badly he wanted to. "First off, that's highly unlikely. Secondly, Ridge and Edge are married. They took a hell of a risk doing this test."

Shadow leaned their way, obviously overhearing their conversation. "It wasn't a risk." He looked clear-eyed and perfectly at peace. "All of you could stand in judgment if you want. Ridge and I have been through too much. We wouldn't give each other up no matter what these results said. We made that decision together, and it wasn't even hard."

Clay felt the power and love behind each word Shadow spoke. His husband meant everything. After half a second of thought, Clay realized he got it. "I wouldn't have judged you. It honestly seems a little unnatural for you two not to be together."

Shadow flashed him a bright smile. "Open the damn results."

At that urging, Clay turned the envelope over and tore open the back. He held his breath as he pulled the paper out from inside. His didn't look like Scout's. It was a letter, and it was from Scout.

Clay,

I'm the one who sneaked Tracker your DNA. While you won't find any lost relatives tonight, you should at least have the option to find any family you may have out there in the future. I asked Tracker not to go looking unless you wanted that. You deserve to have a choice. I've always had a home country and brothers. I won't say they aren't blood. We've shed more blood for each other than anyone born from the same womb ever could. According to Tracker, considering the high percentage of Italian DNA, it's possible you could have some six degrees of separation thing with Beau's family tree. That might be one reason you were placed with him. Anyhow, I know it's not much, but that's all I could offer. No matter how you feel about looking into your history, you'll always still have me at the end of the day. I'm your family. On that note, would you marry me? It'd be kind of cool if you did.

A laugh burst from Clay over that last sentence. The sound died when he looked Scout's way. Scout held a ring and had all the hope in the world in his eyes. The collective silence had Clay casting a quick glance around the room. Everyone stared at them as if holding their breath.

Clay met Scout's pleading stare. "As if I'd say no." He snatched the ring from Scout before it disappeared. Clay was scared as fuck this was all a dream. He stuck that ring on his finger so damn fast, he didn't even get a good look at it. All he wanted was Scout. In an in-stant, he had the kiss he wanted while clapping and congratulations went up around them.

"I really hope you want to get married tomorrow," Clay said against Scout's lips, trying to keep the conversation between them.

"Fuck yeah."

Clay laughed as Scout overwhelmed him with all the public displays of affection. Maybe they were crazy. Clay gave less than zero fucks if they were. Like Shadow had said, everyone could stand on their fucking judgment if they wanted. His heart was right here. He wanted everyone to know it.

Keep an eye out for the next Killers Inc., *Tracker.*

About the Author

CHARITY PARKERSON IS AN award-winning and multi-published author with several companies. Born with no filter from her brain to her mouth, she decided to take this odd quirk and insert it in her characters. One of her greatest loves is writing morally gray characters. You'll find them scattered throughout her hundreds of titles.

*Nine-time Readers' Favorite Award Winner

*2015 Passionate Plume Award Finalist

*2013 Reviewers' Choice Award Winner

*2012 ARRA Finalist for Favorite Paranormal Romance

*Five-time winner of The Mistress of the Darkpath

Connect with her online:

*Sign up for her newsletter: https://bit.ly/charityparkersonnewsletter

*Join her readers' group on Facebook: http://bit.ly/CharitysTribe

*Website: https://www.charityparkerson.com

*A list of her social media accounts and giveaways all in one place: http://hy.page/charityparkerson